Hello Kitty
FASHION ♥ MUSIC WONDERLAND

Jacob Chabot
Victoria Maderna
Ian McGinty

Hello Kitty

FASHION•MUSIC WONDERLAND

"Pretty in Pink"   Story by Traci N. Todd, art by Victoria Maderna

"High Note!"   Story by Traci N. Todd, art by Ian McGinty,
colors by Michael E. Wiggam

"Wonderland"   Story by Traci N. Todd and Jacob Chabot, inspired by
Alice's Adventures in Wonderland by Lewis Carroll,
colors by Michael E. Wiggam

Cover A Art   Jacob Chabot
Cover B Art   Victoria Maderna
Design   Shawn Carrico
Editor   Traci N. Todd

Printed in the U.S.A.

Published by VIZ Media, LLC
P.O. Box 77010
San Francisco, CA 94107

10 9 8 7 6 5 4 3 2
First printing, 2013
Second printing, March 2015

www.viz.com

CONTENTS

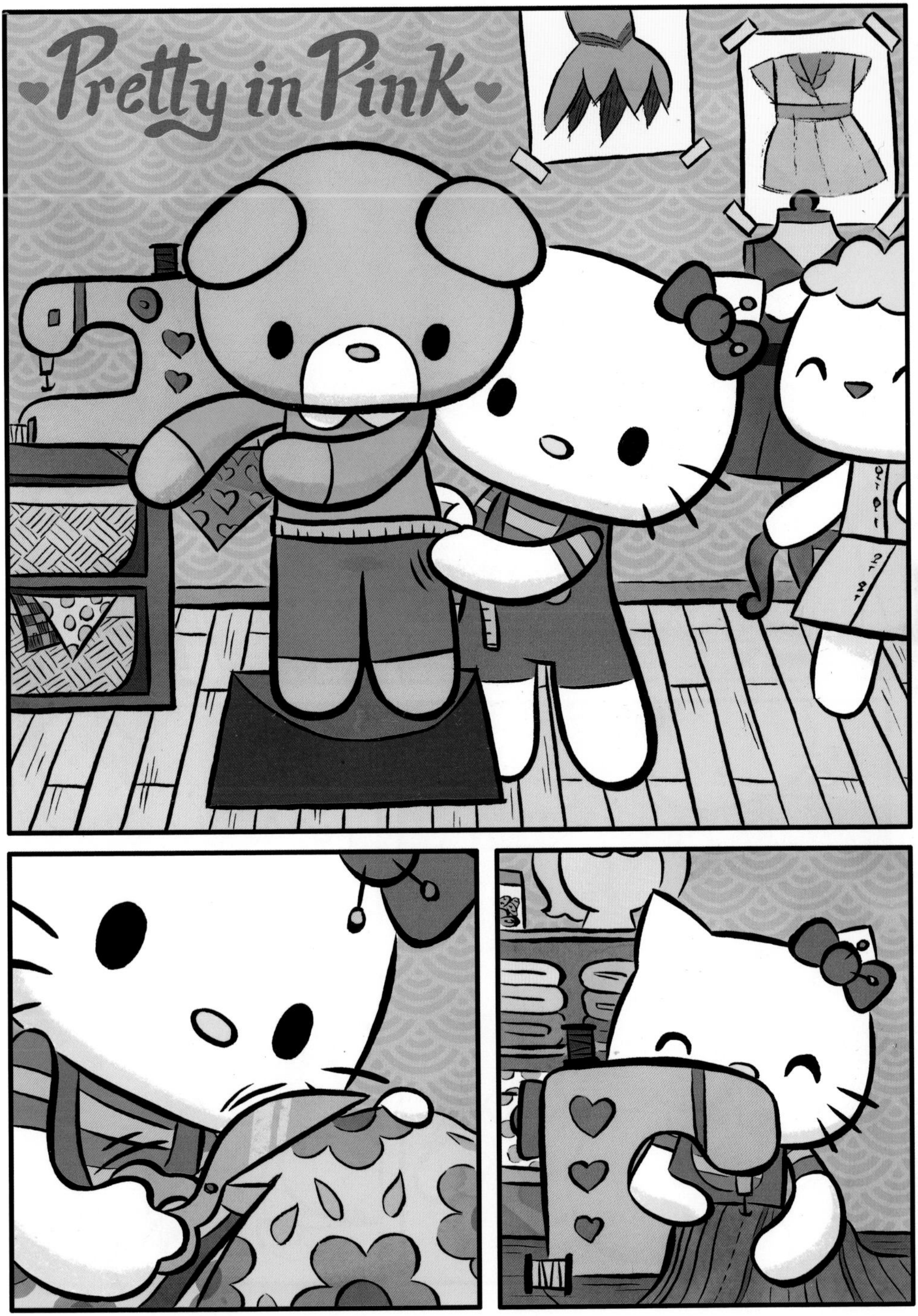
Pretty in Pink

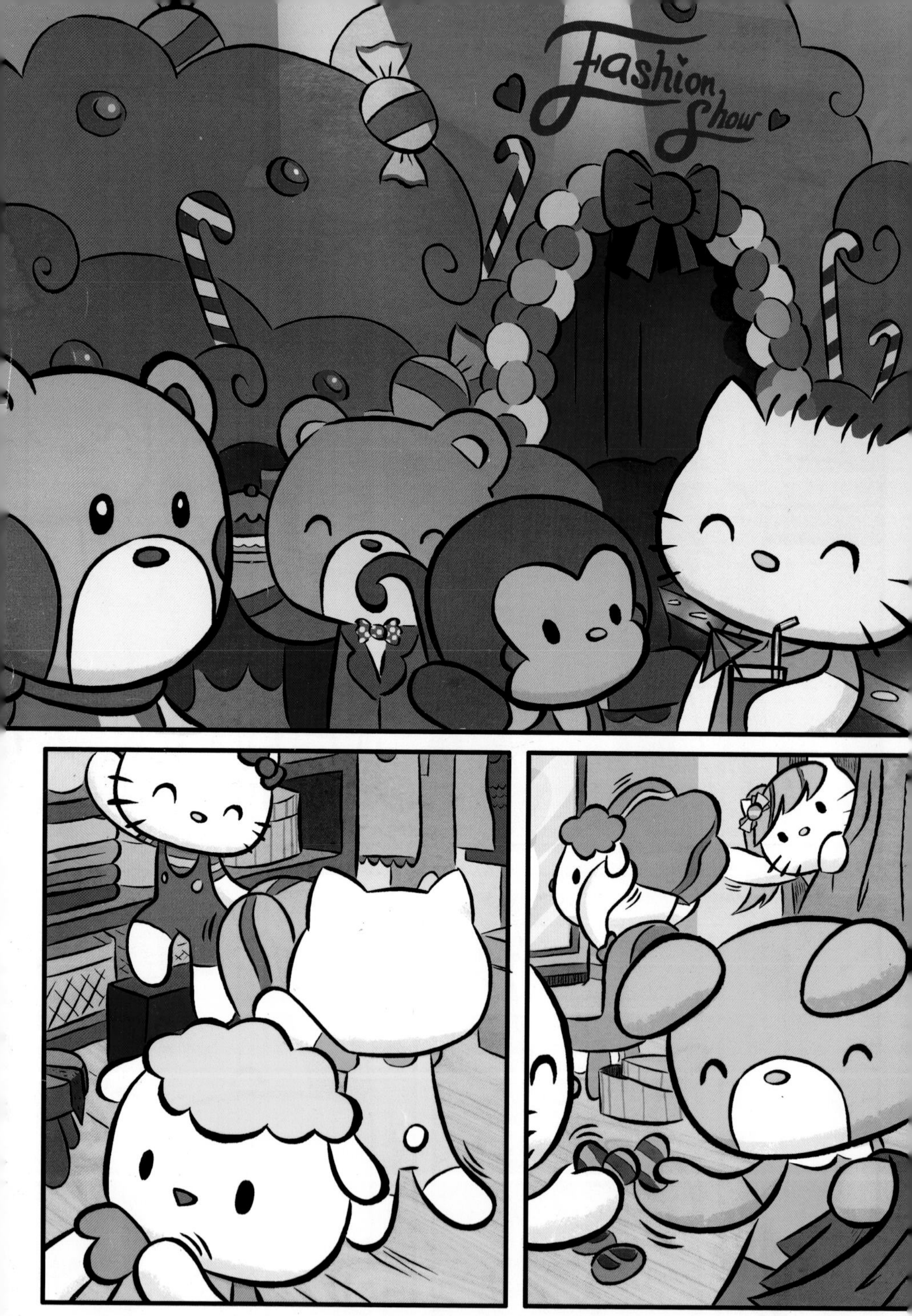
Fashion Show

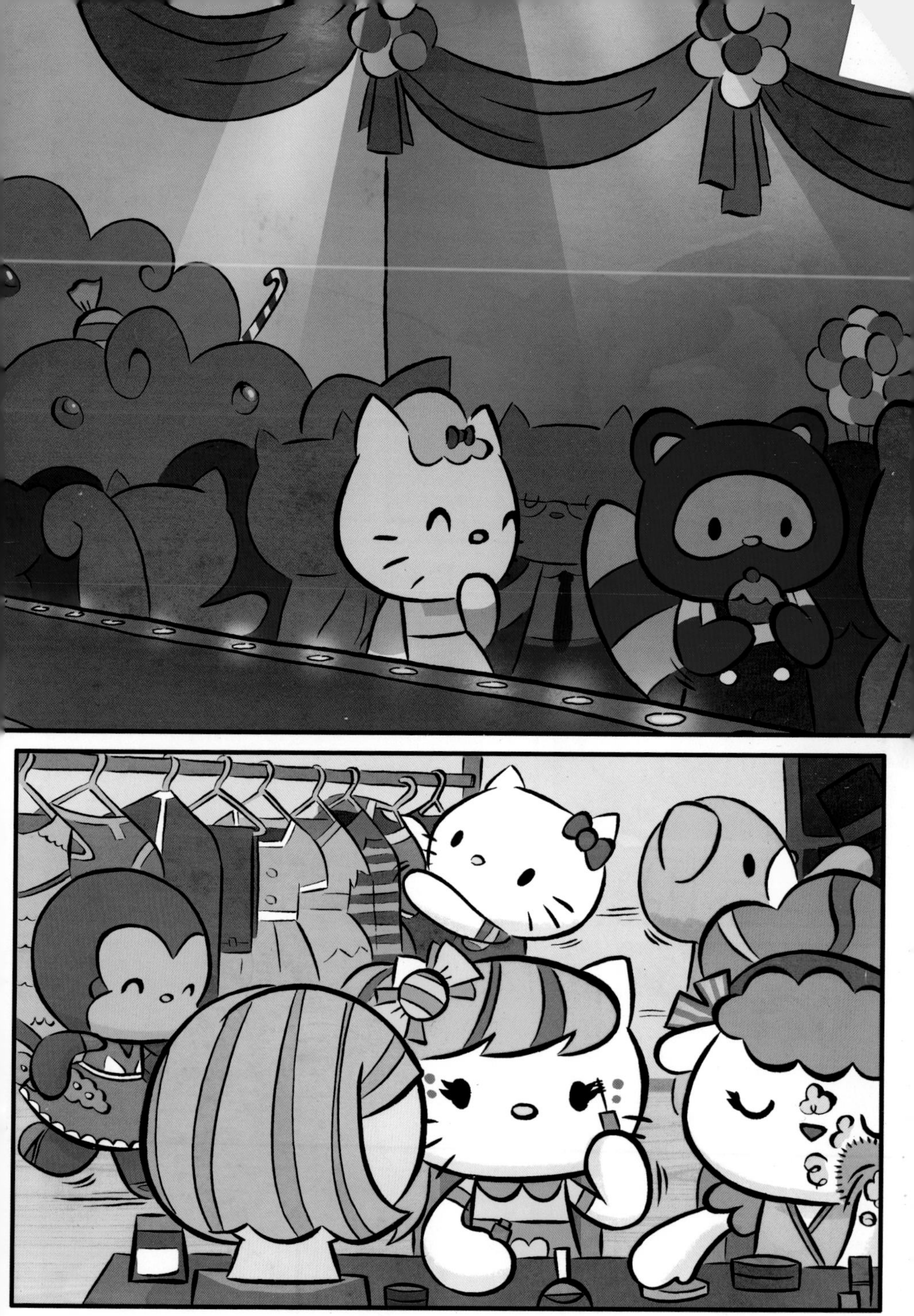

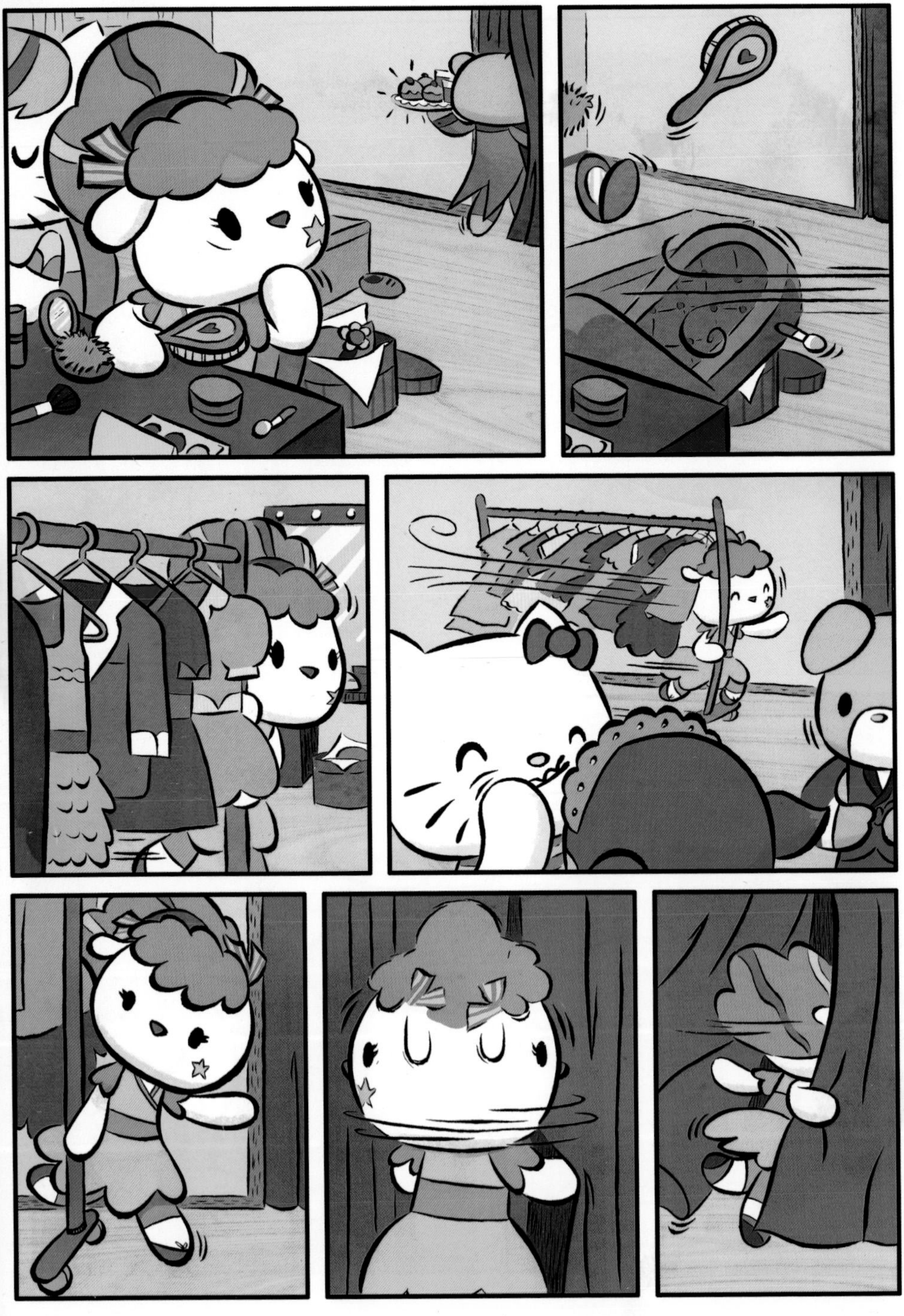

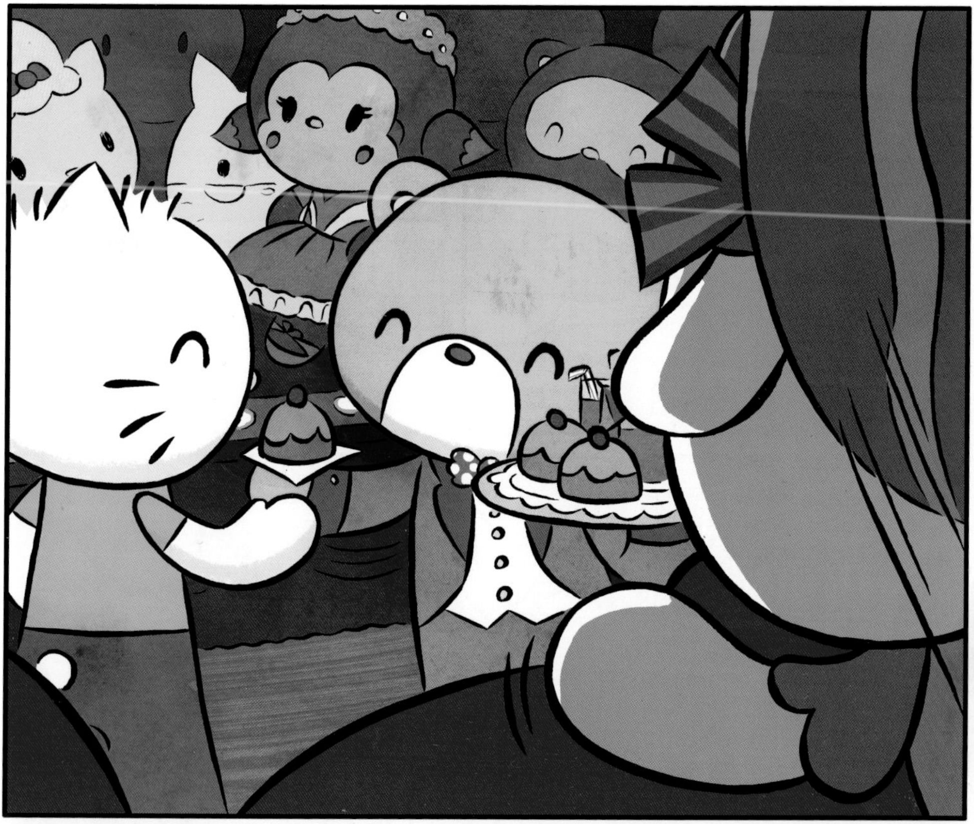

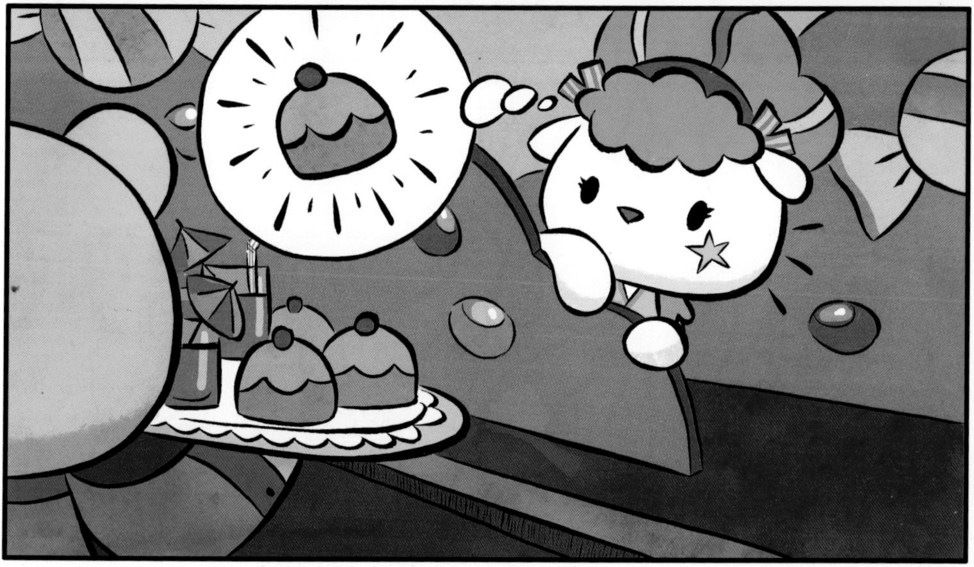

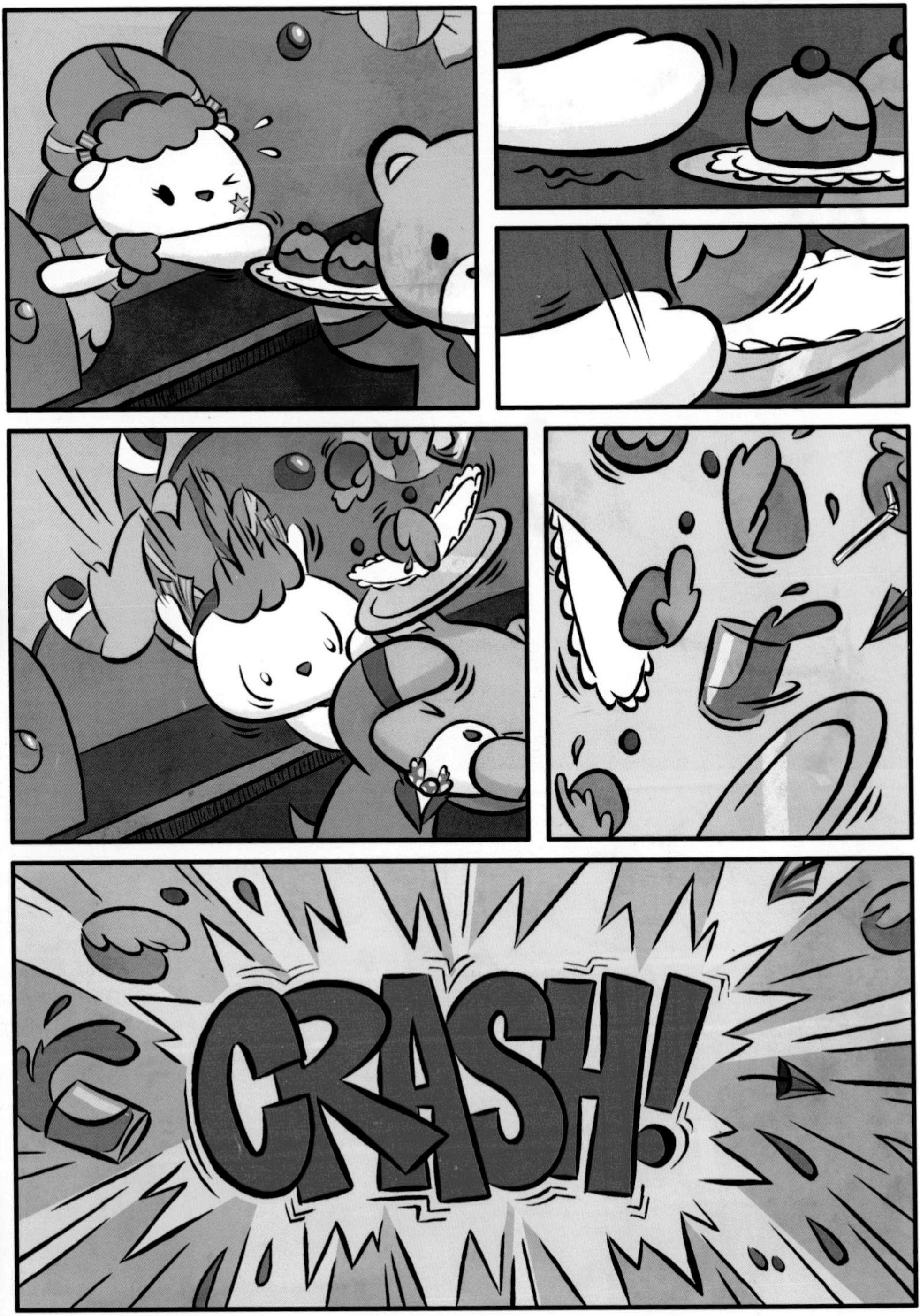
CRASH!

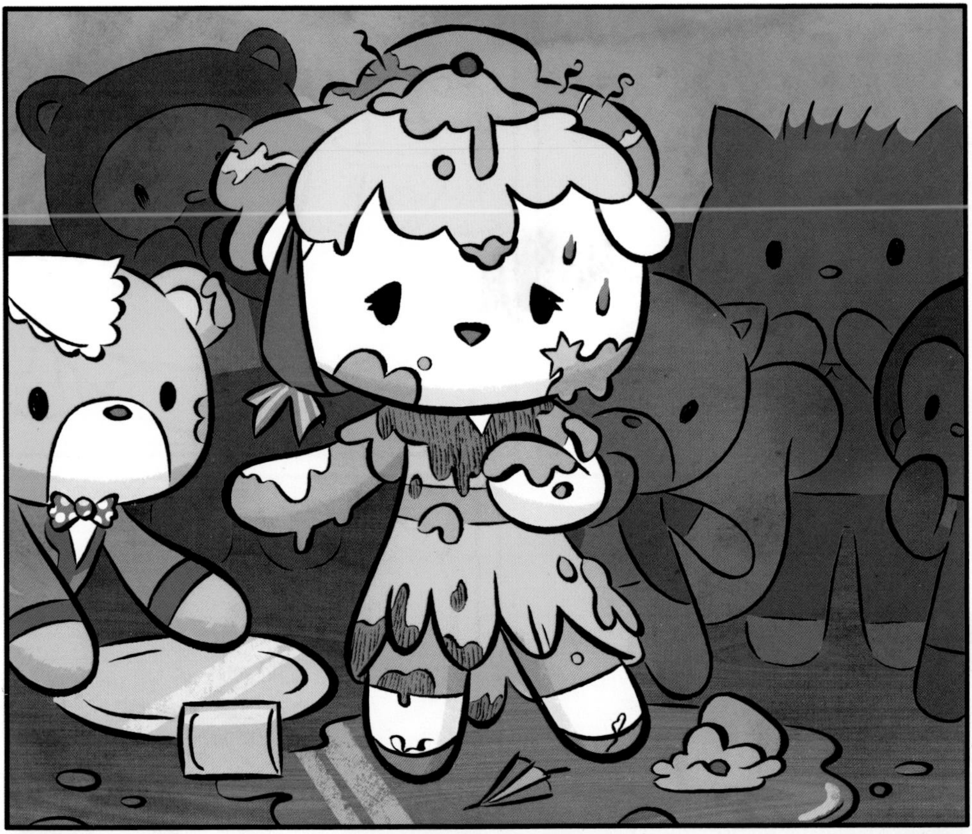

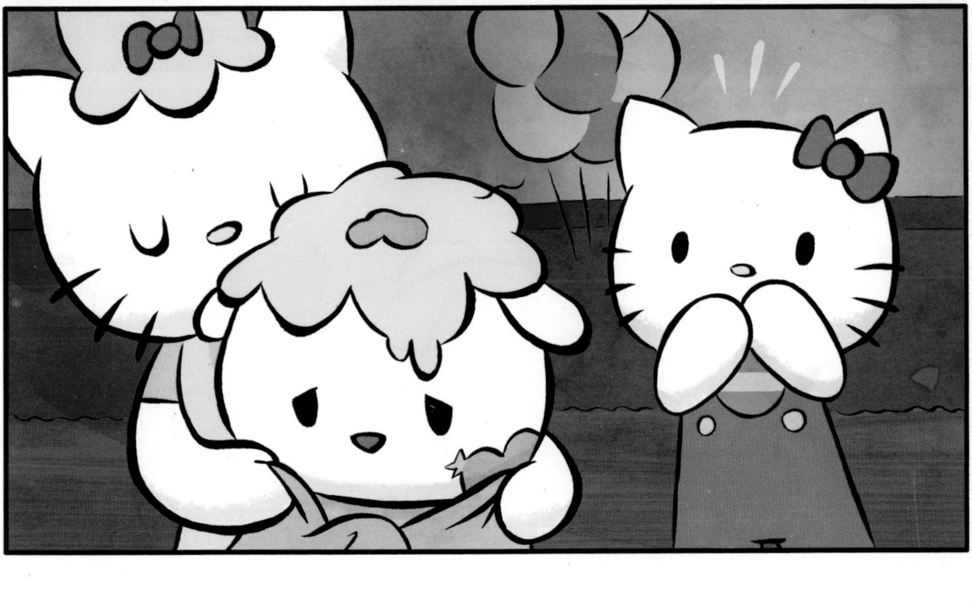

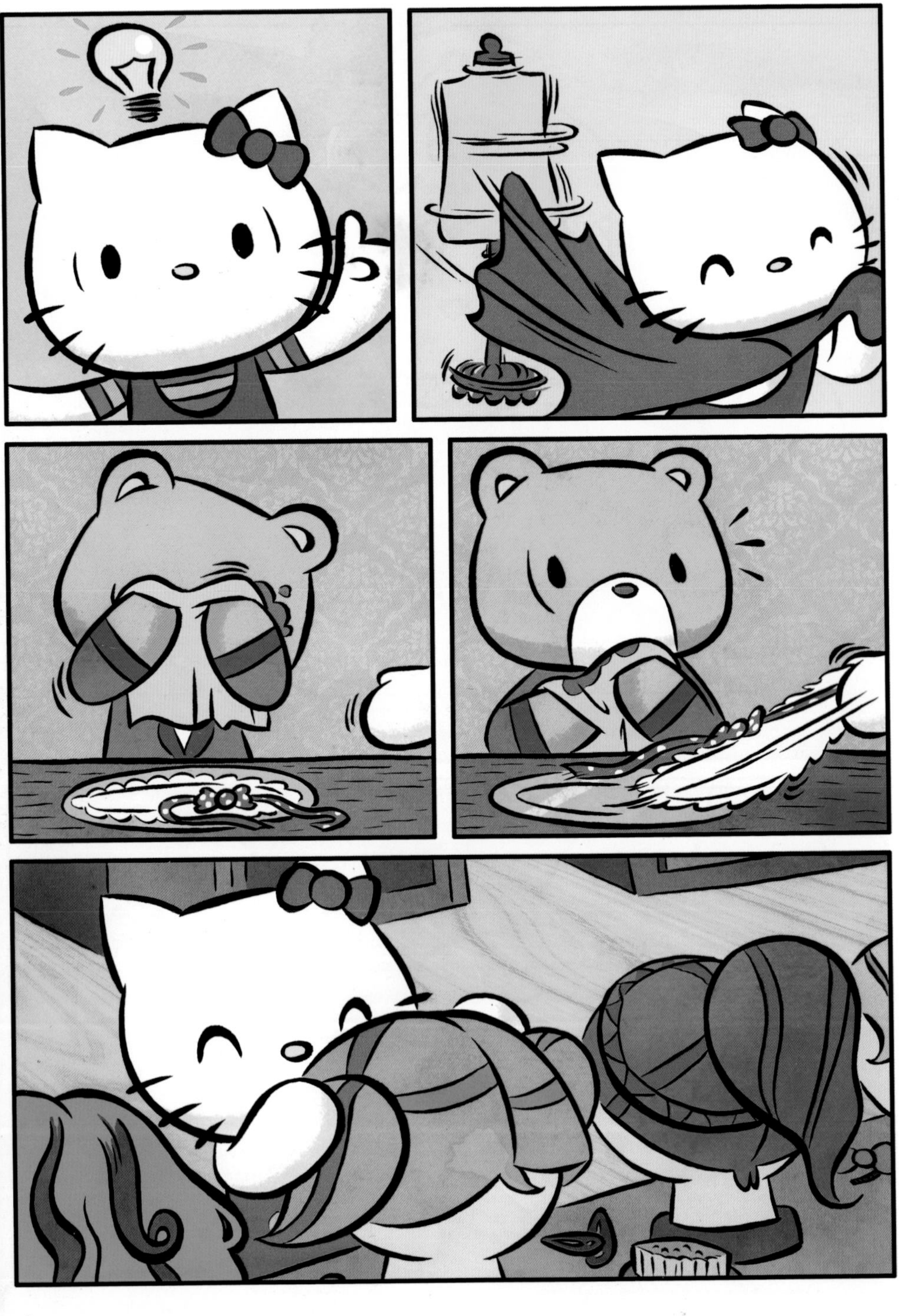

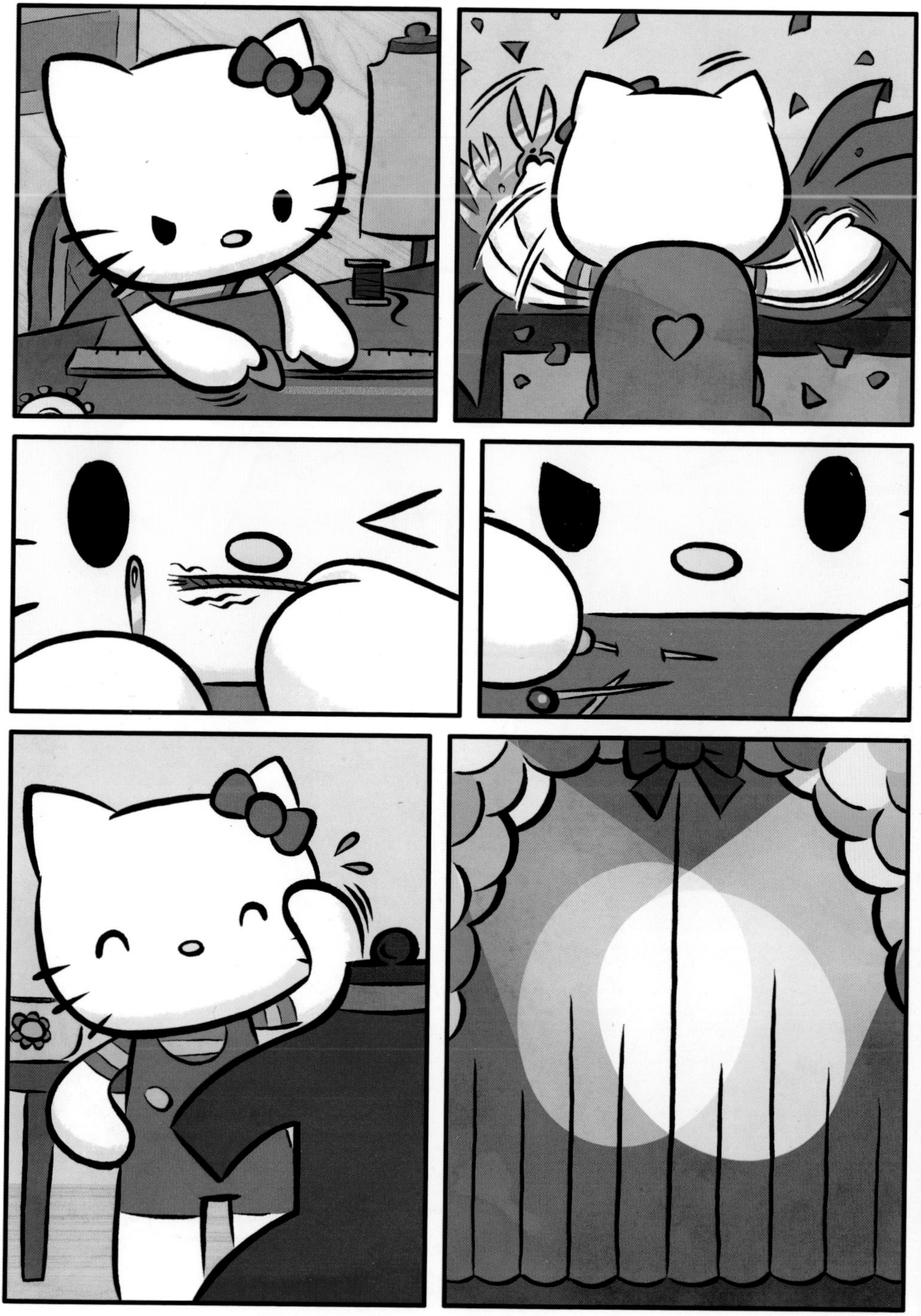

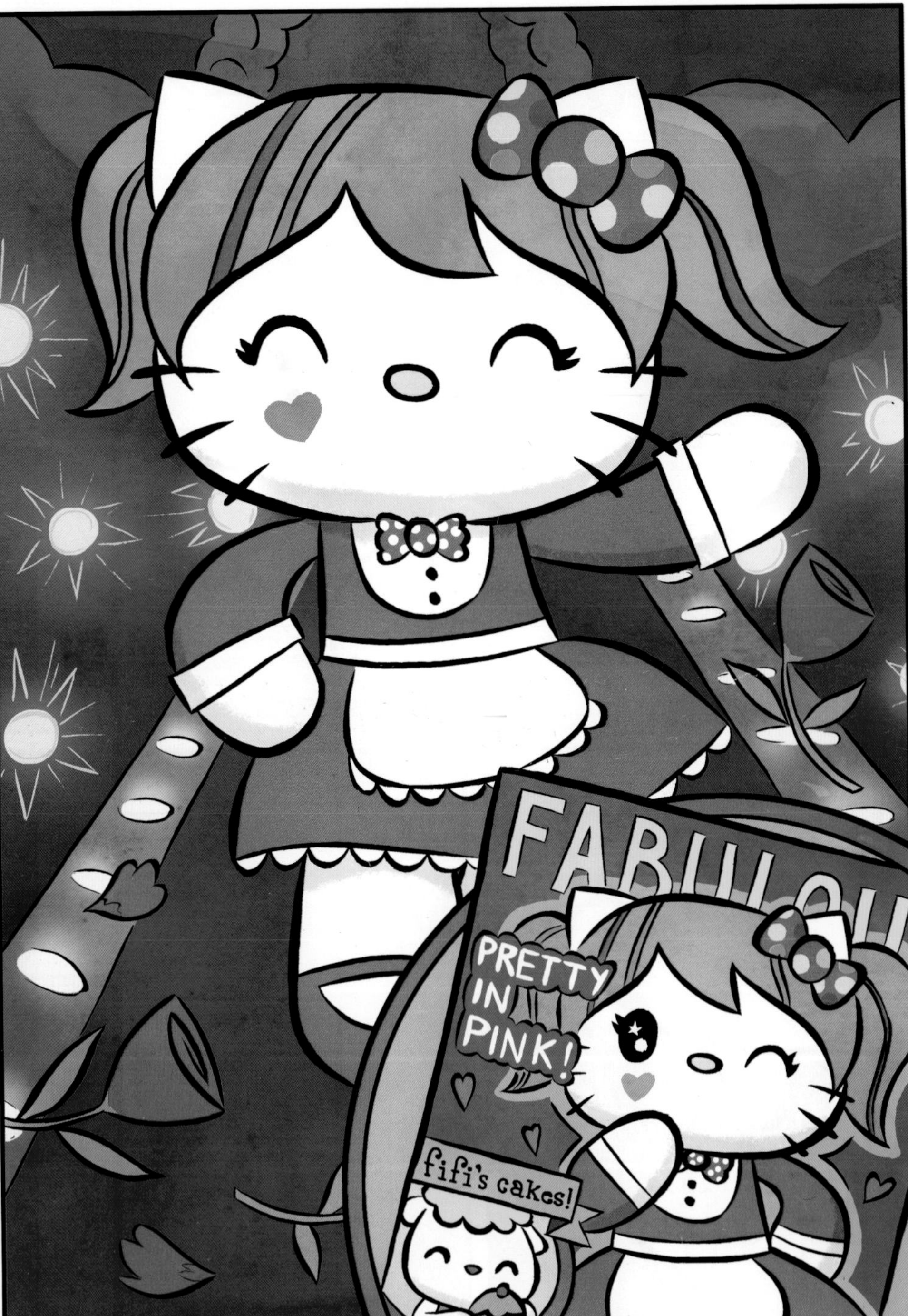
FABULOU
PRETTY IN PINK!
fifi's cakes!

end!

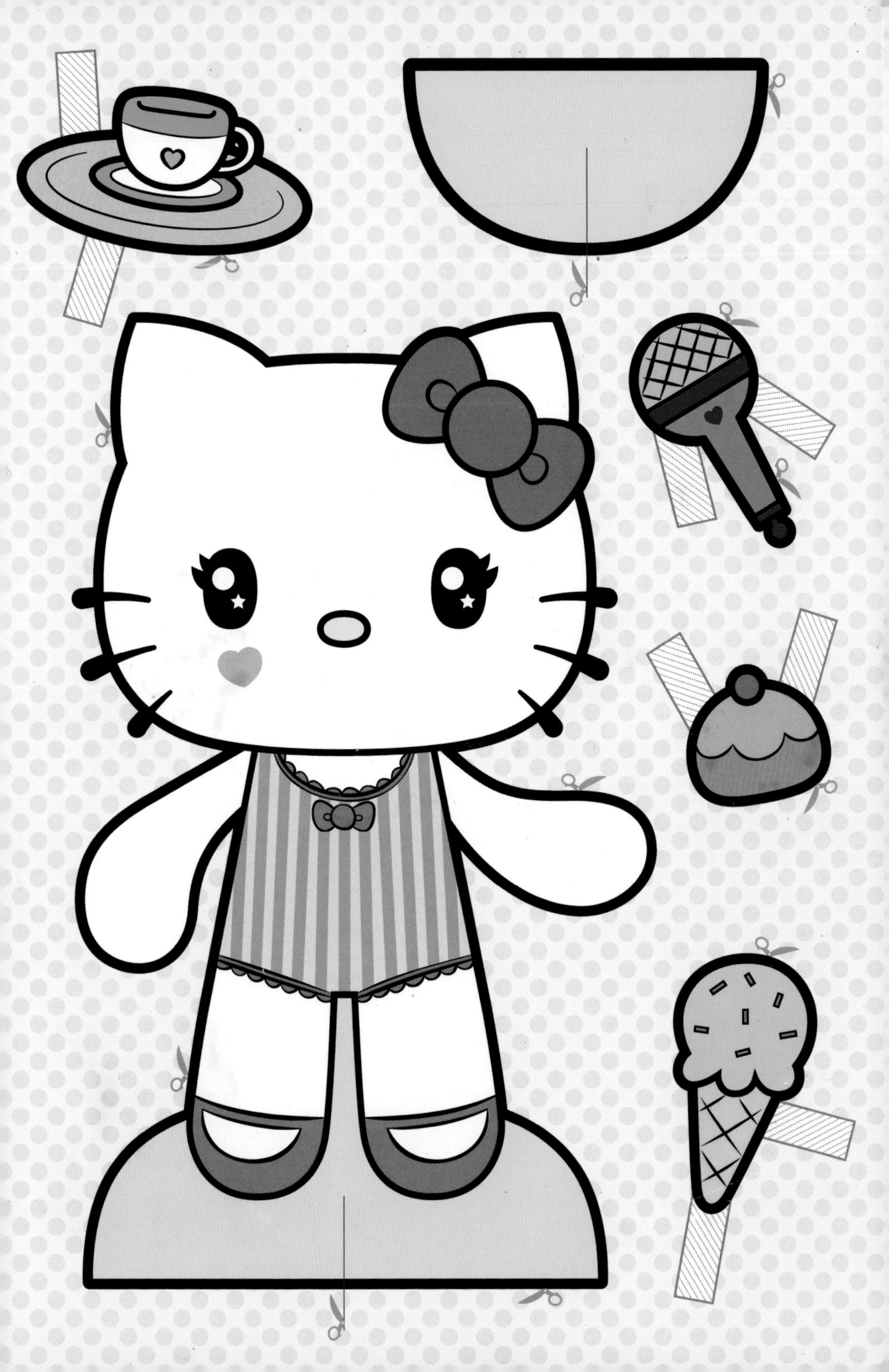

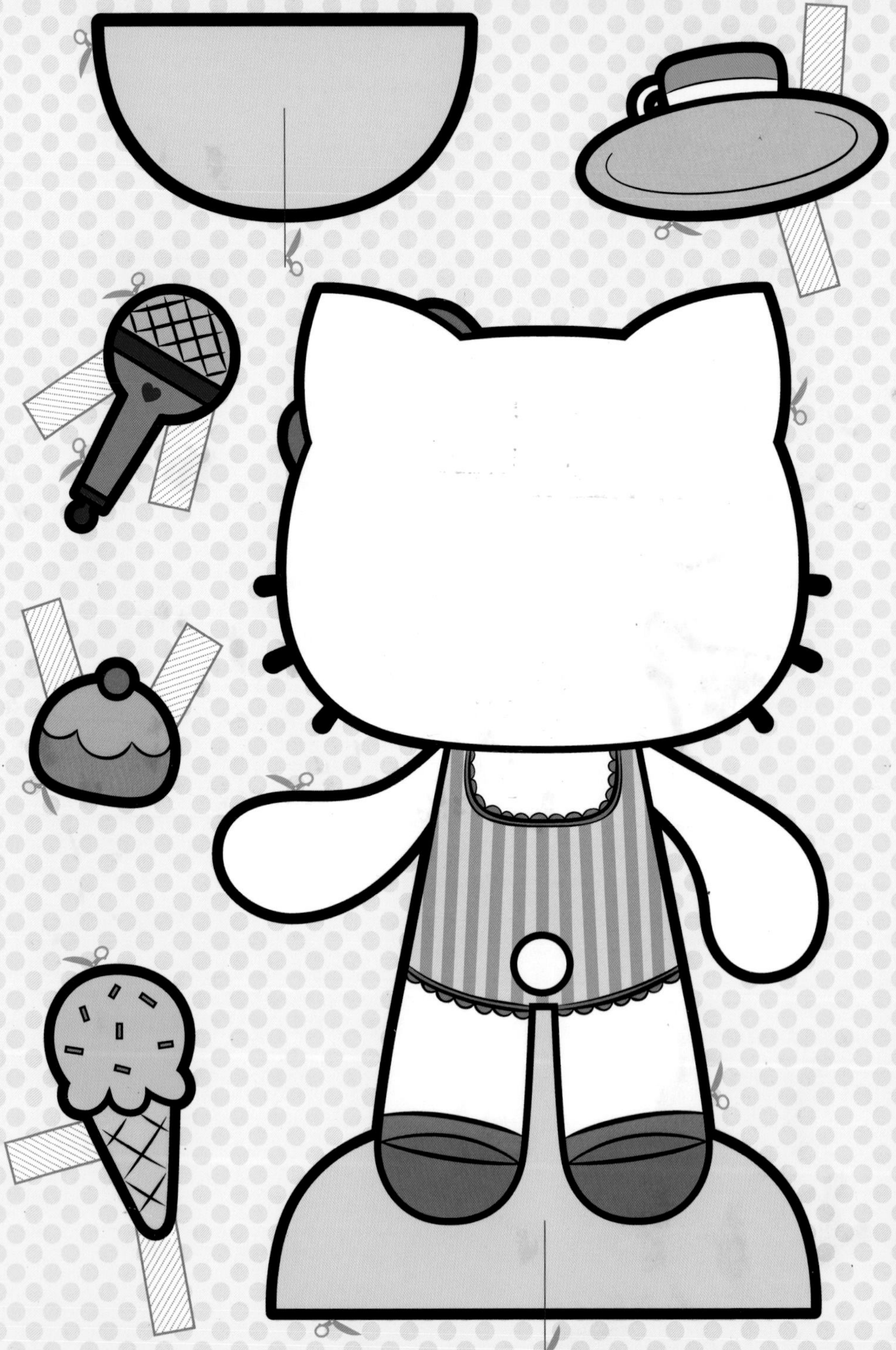

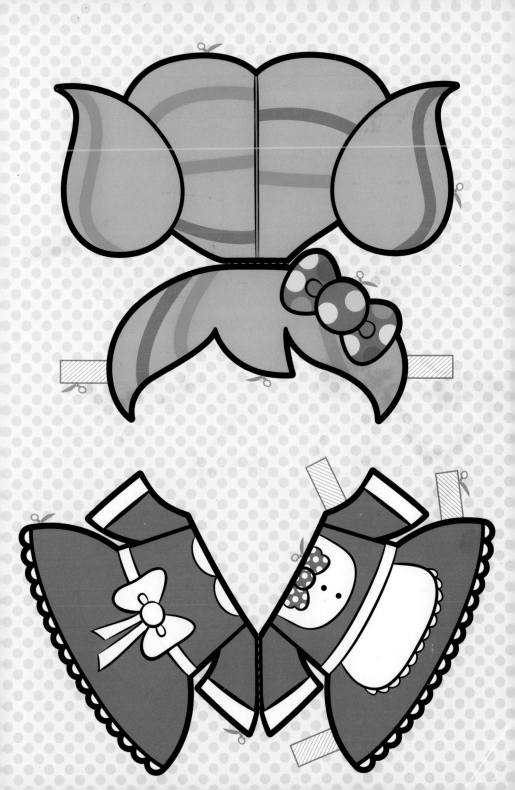

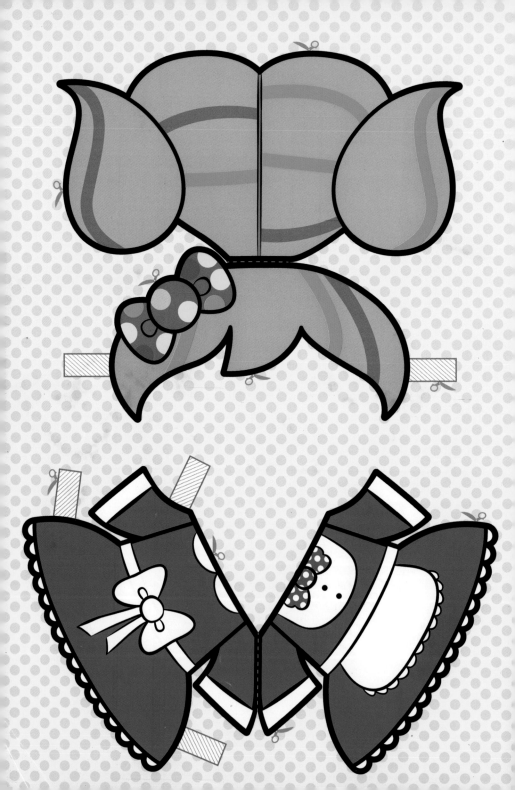

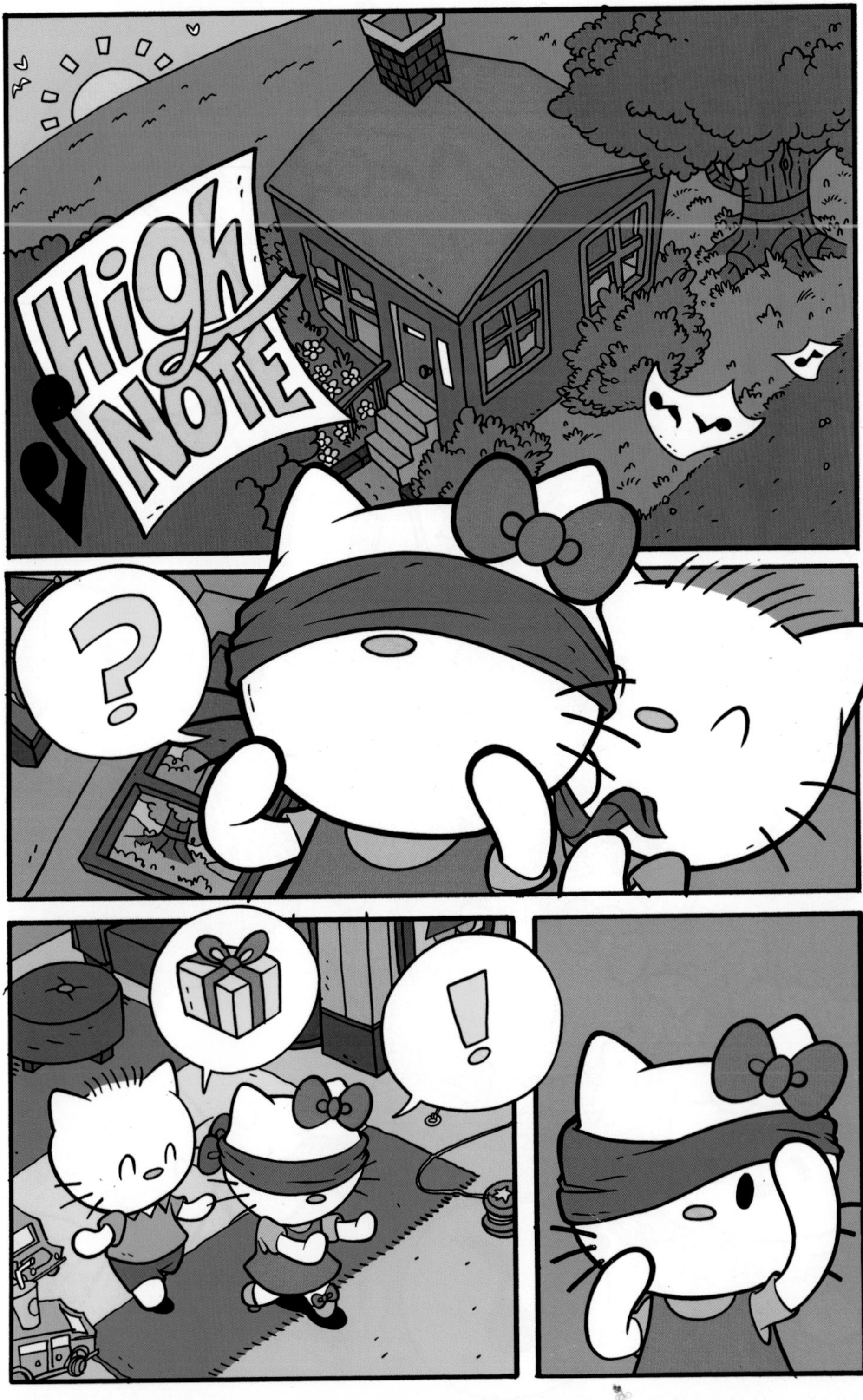
High Note
?
!

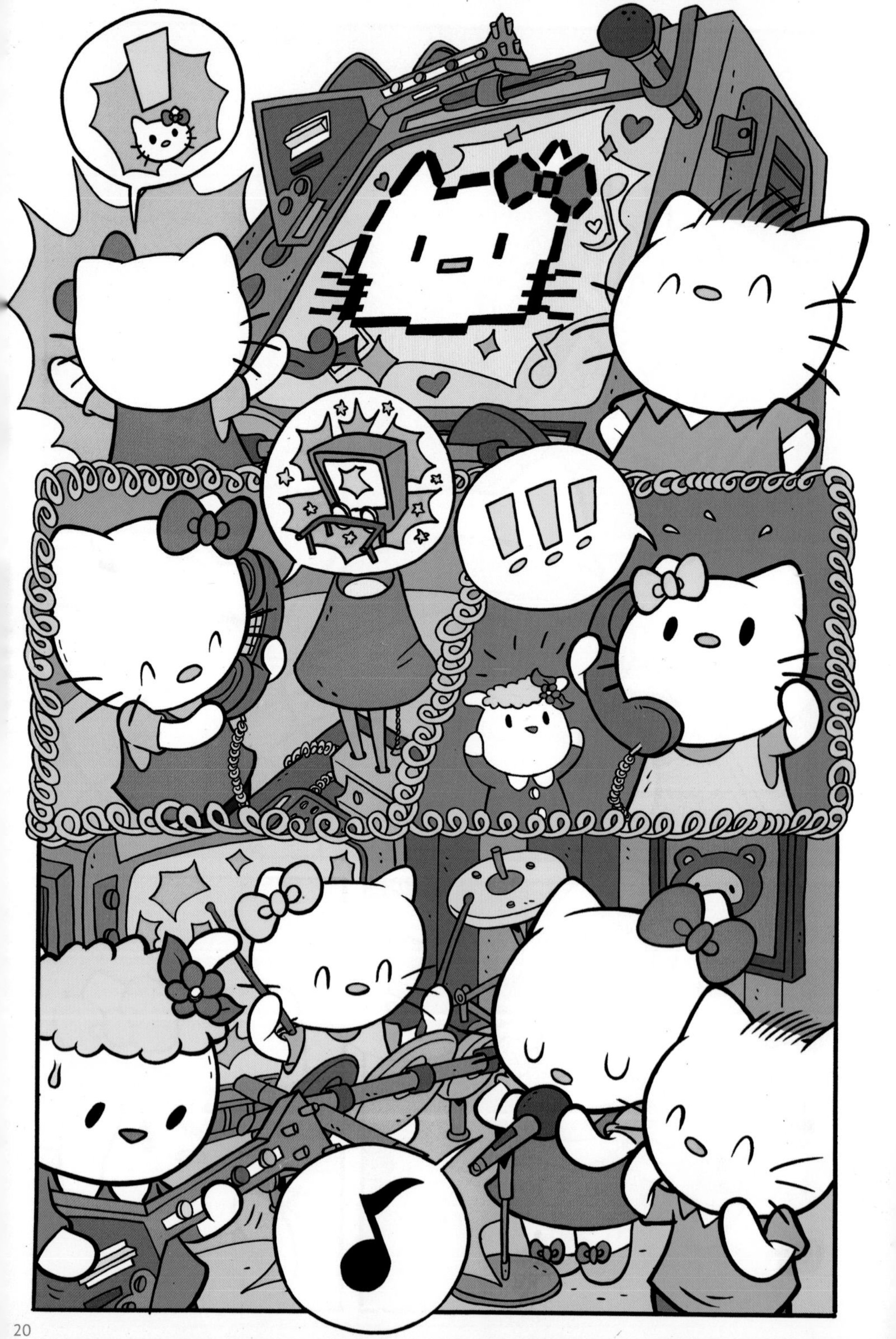

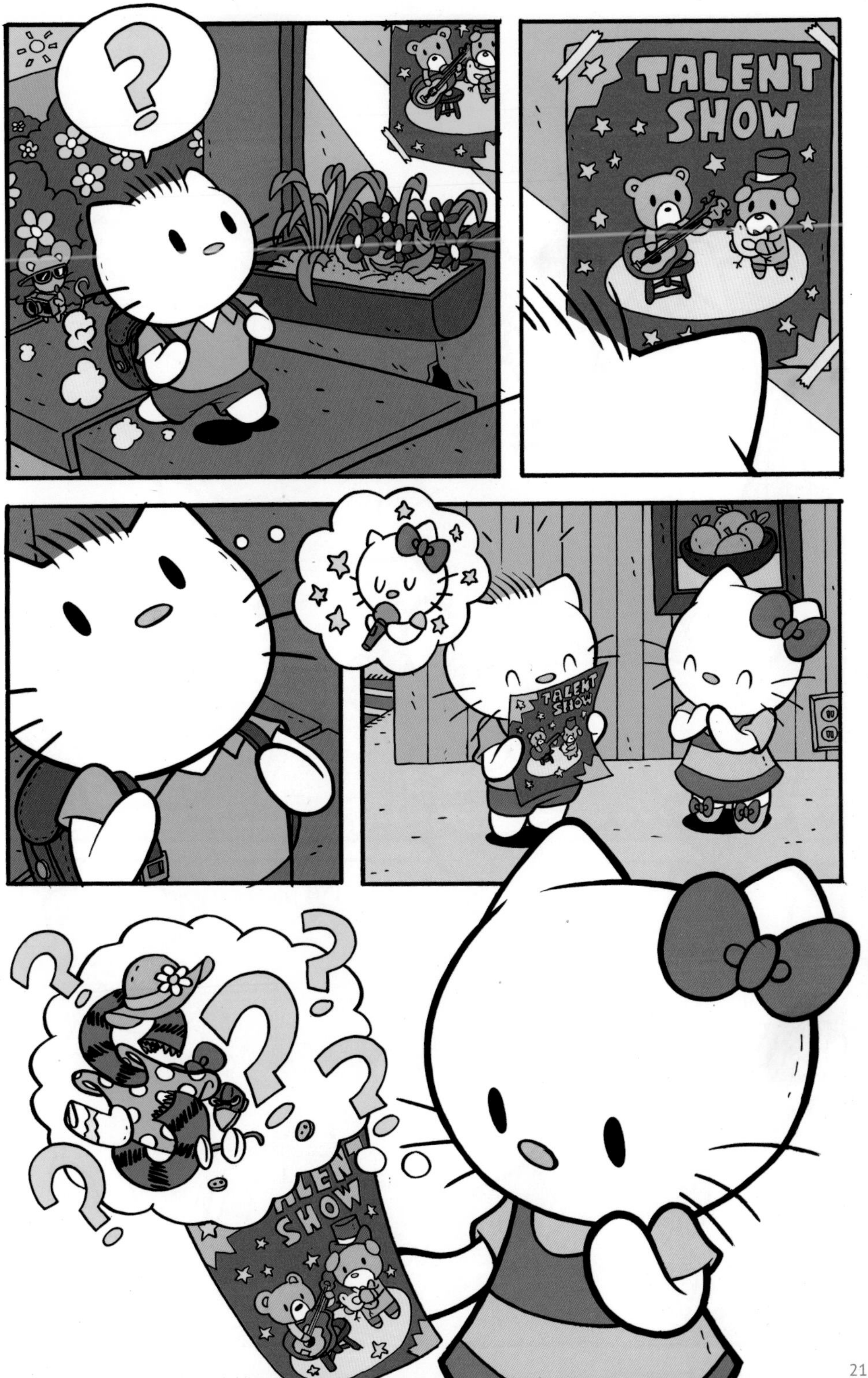
?
TALENT SHOW
TALENT SHOW
TALENT SHOW

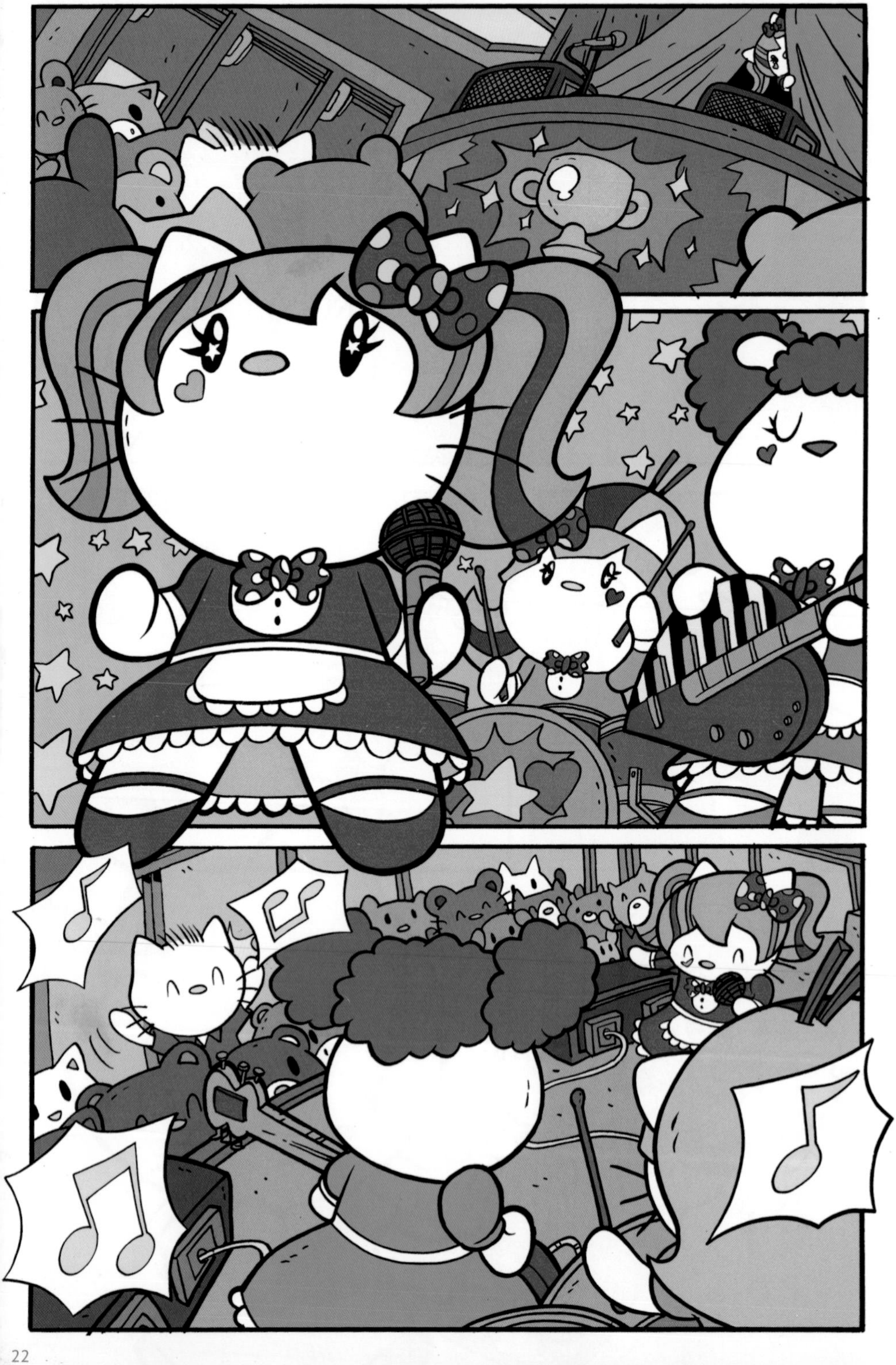

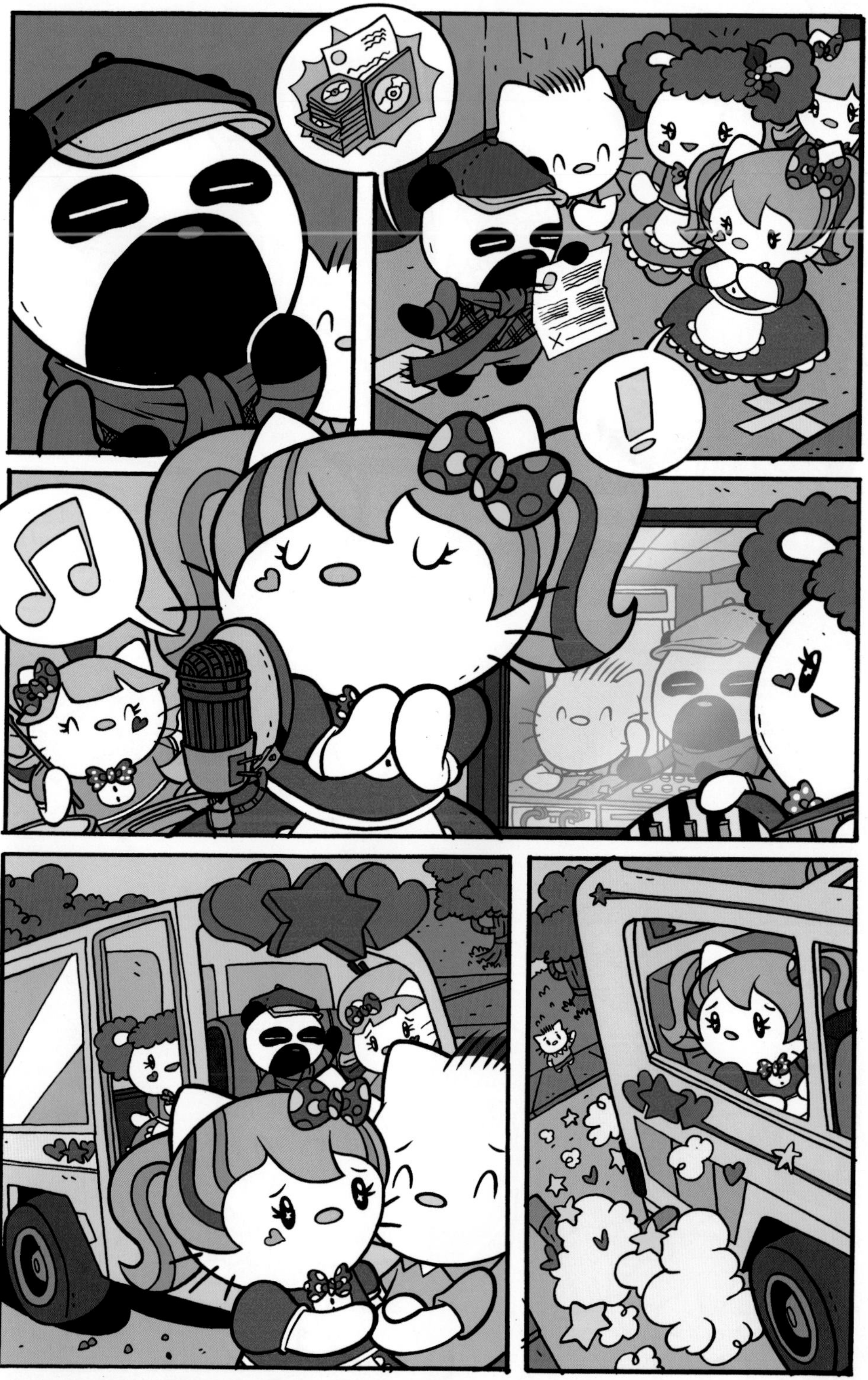

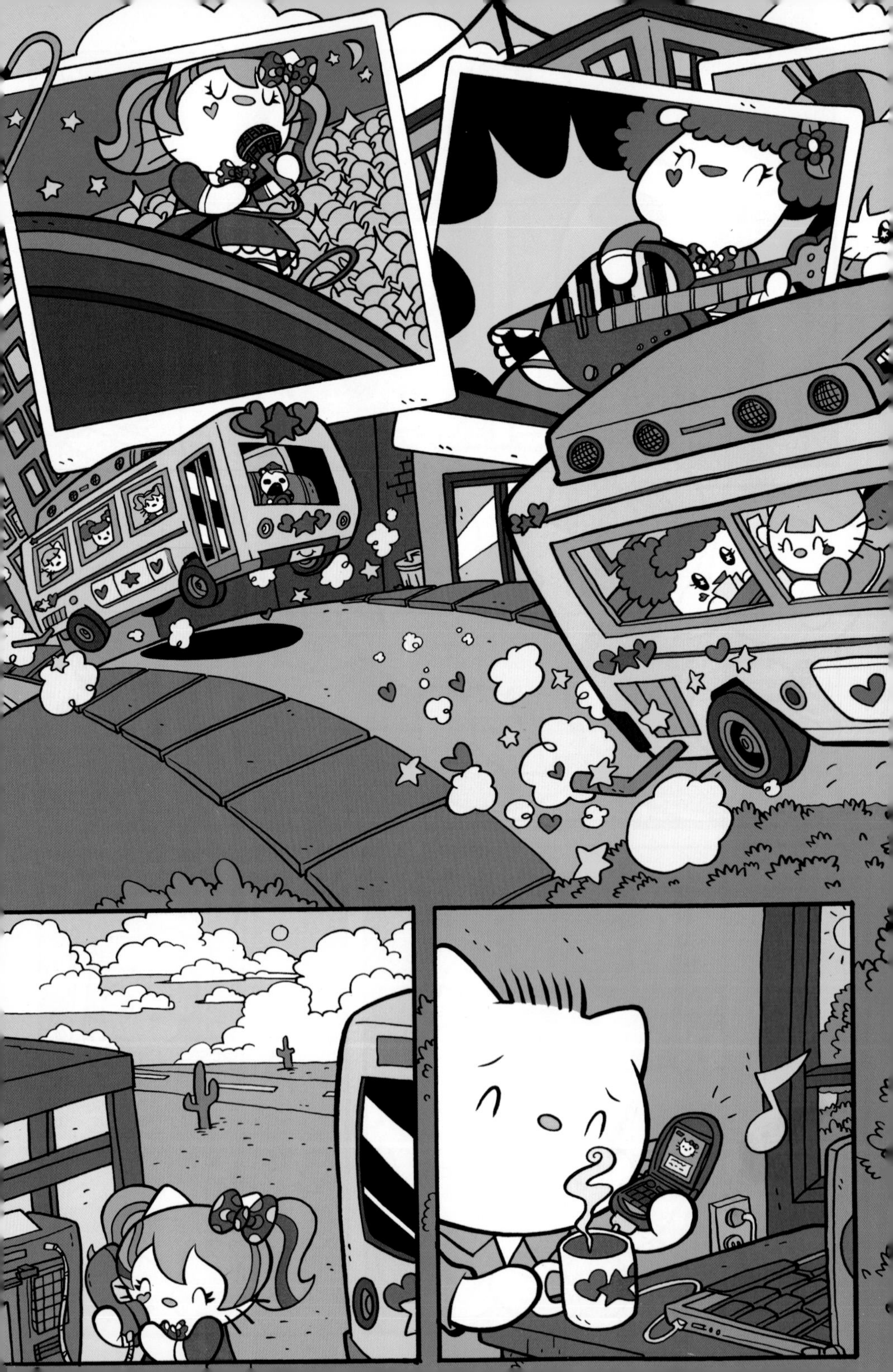

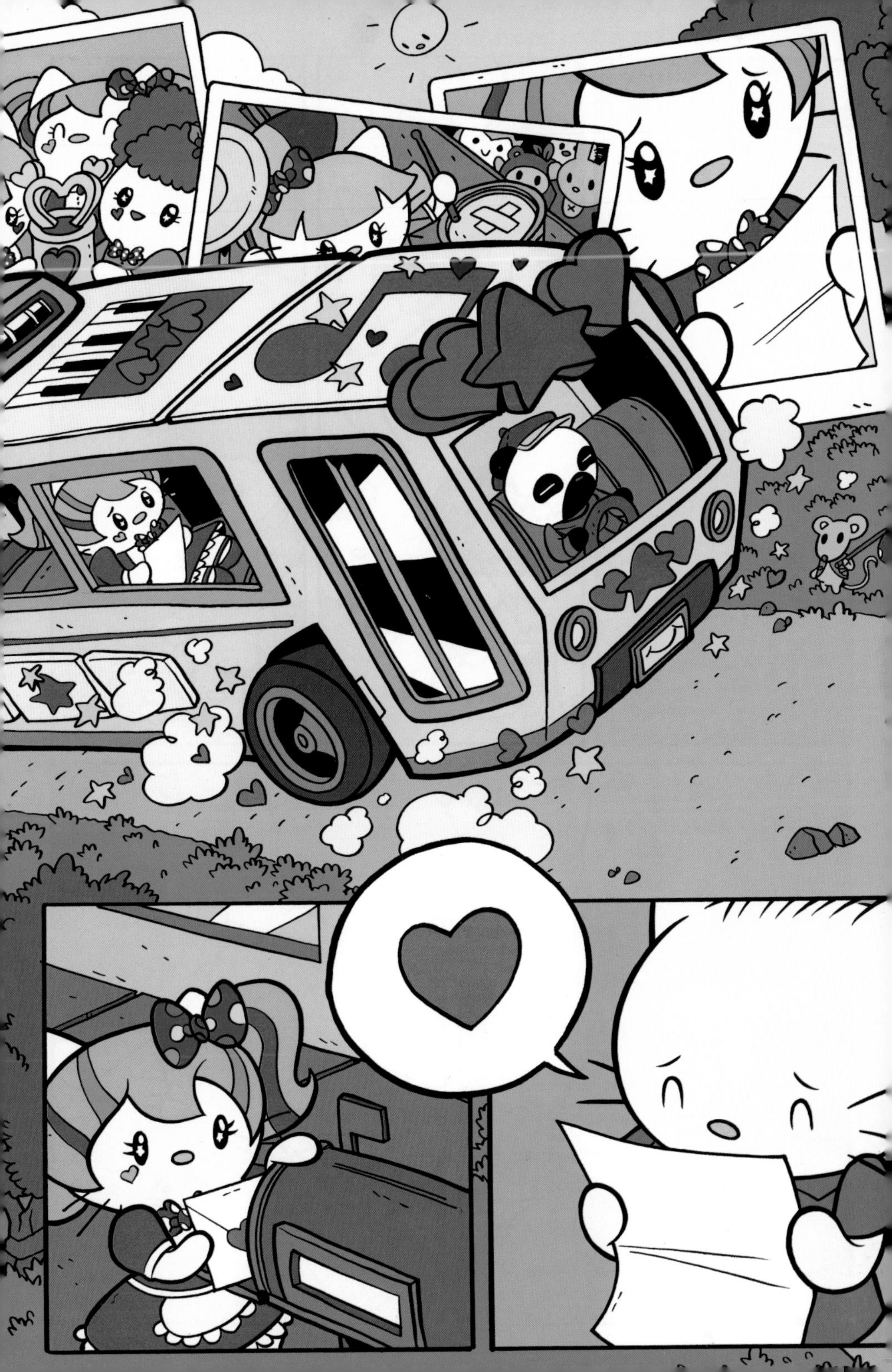

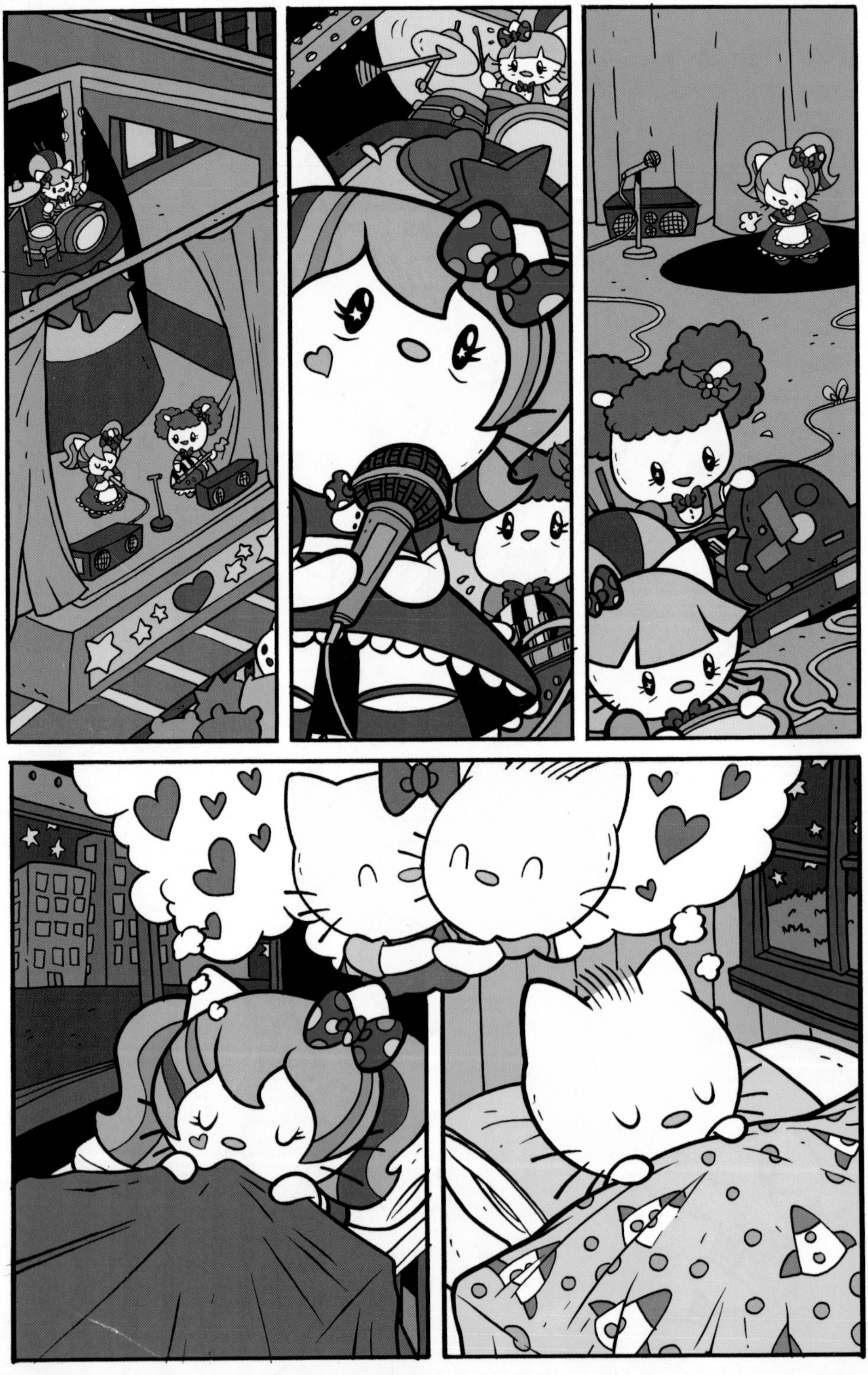

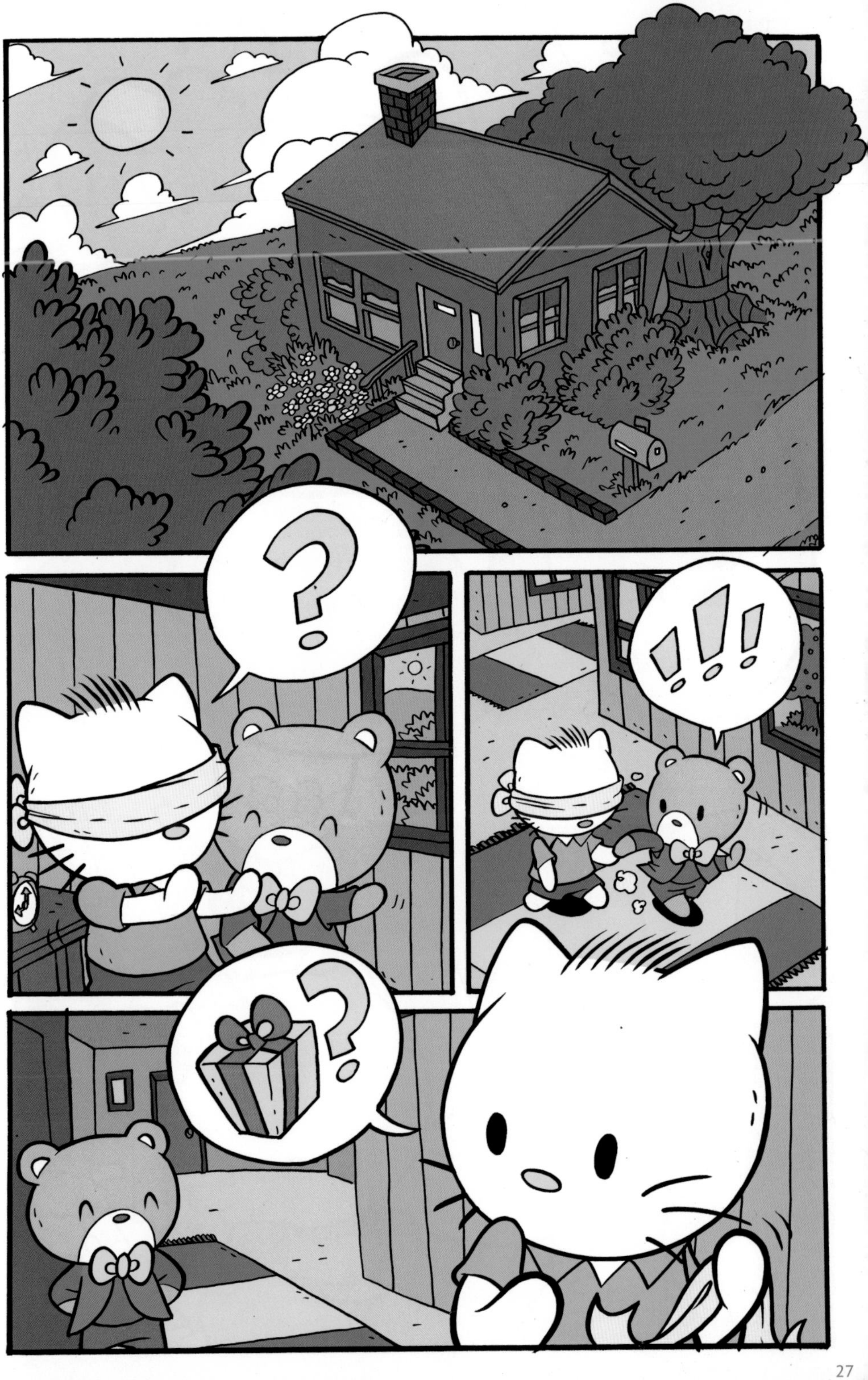
?
!!!
?

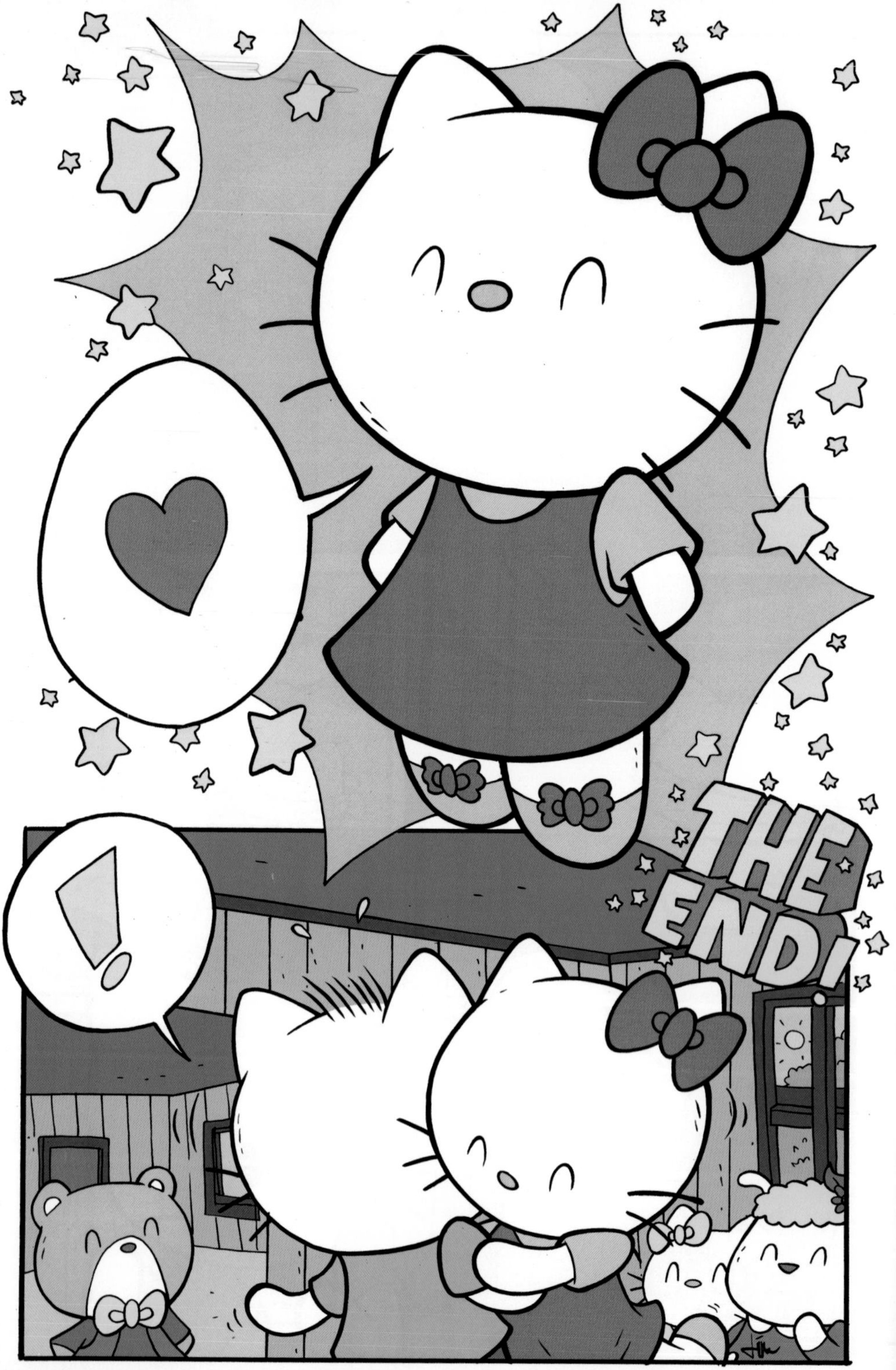
!
THE END!

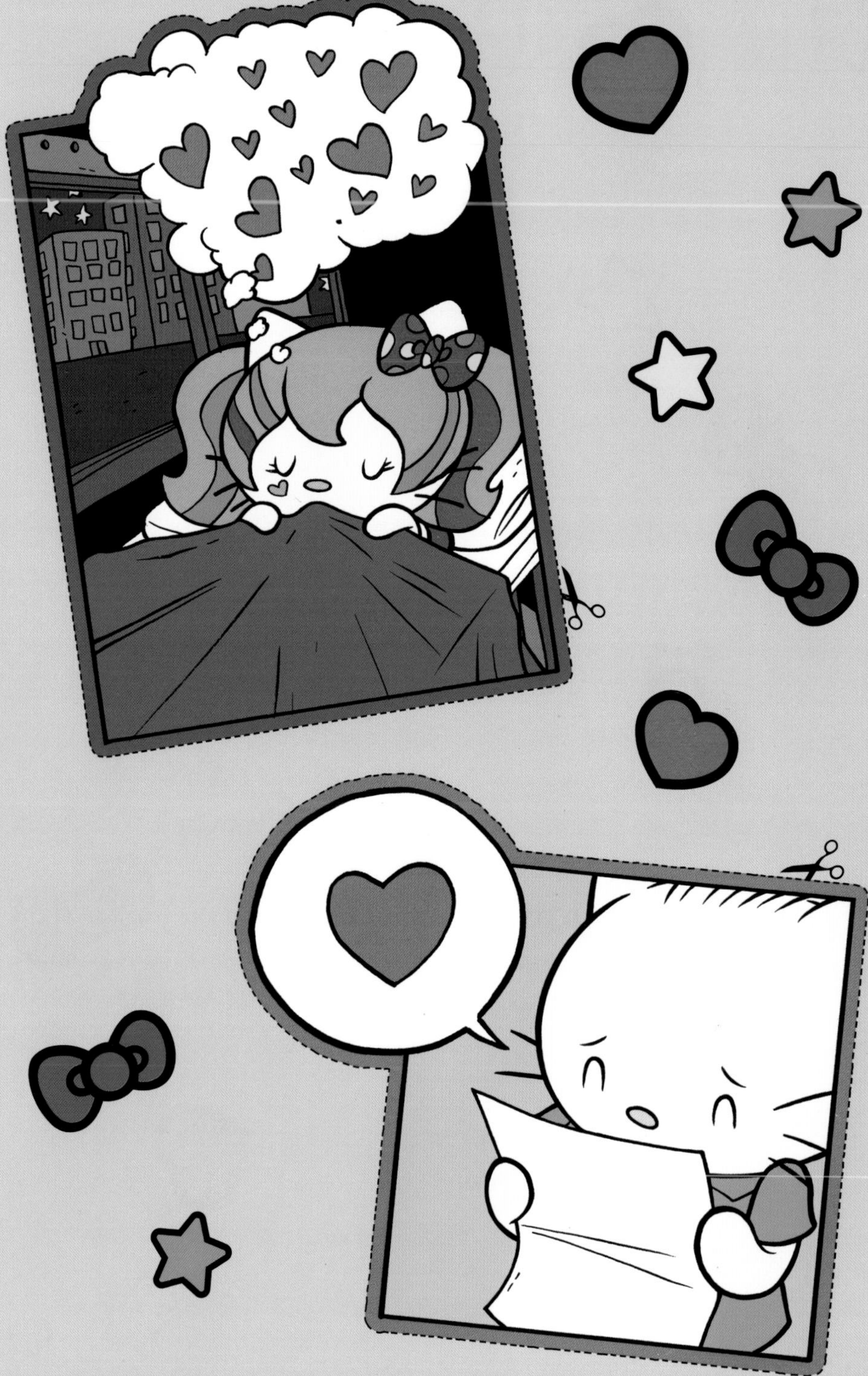

**Thinking
of you!**

....
....
....
....
....
....
....
....
....
....
....
....

Thinking of you!

....
....
....
....
....
....
....
....

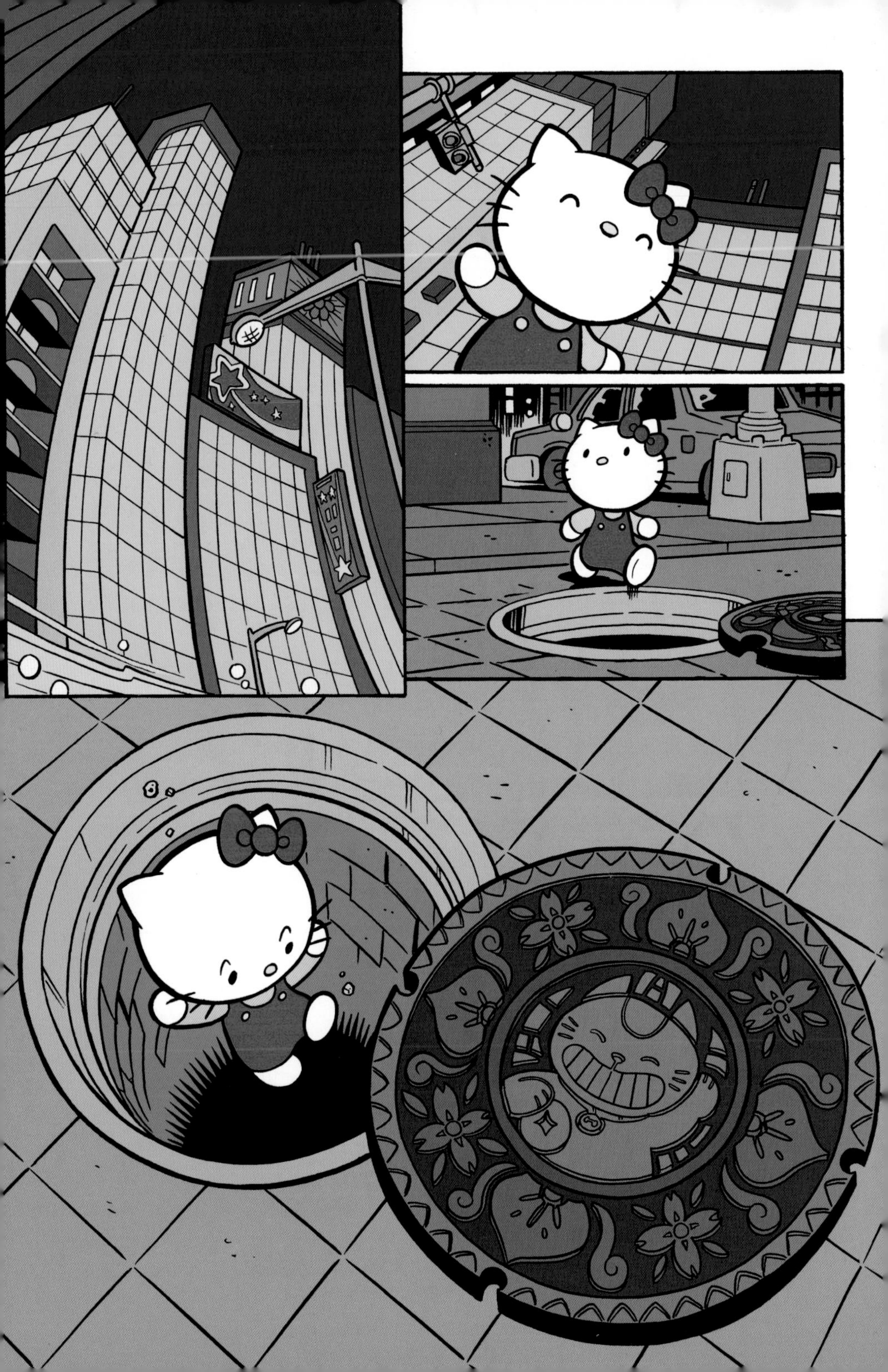

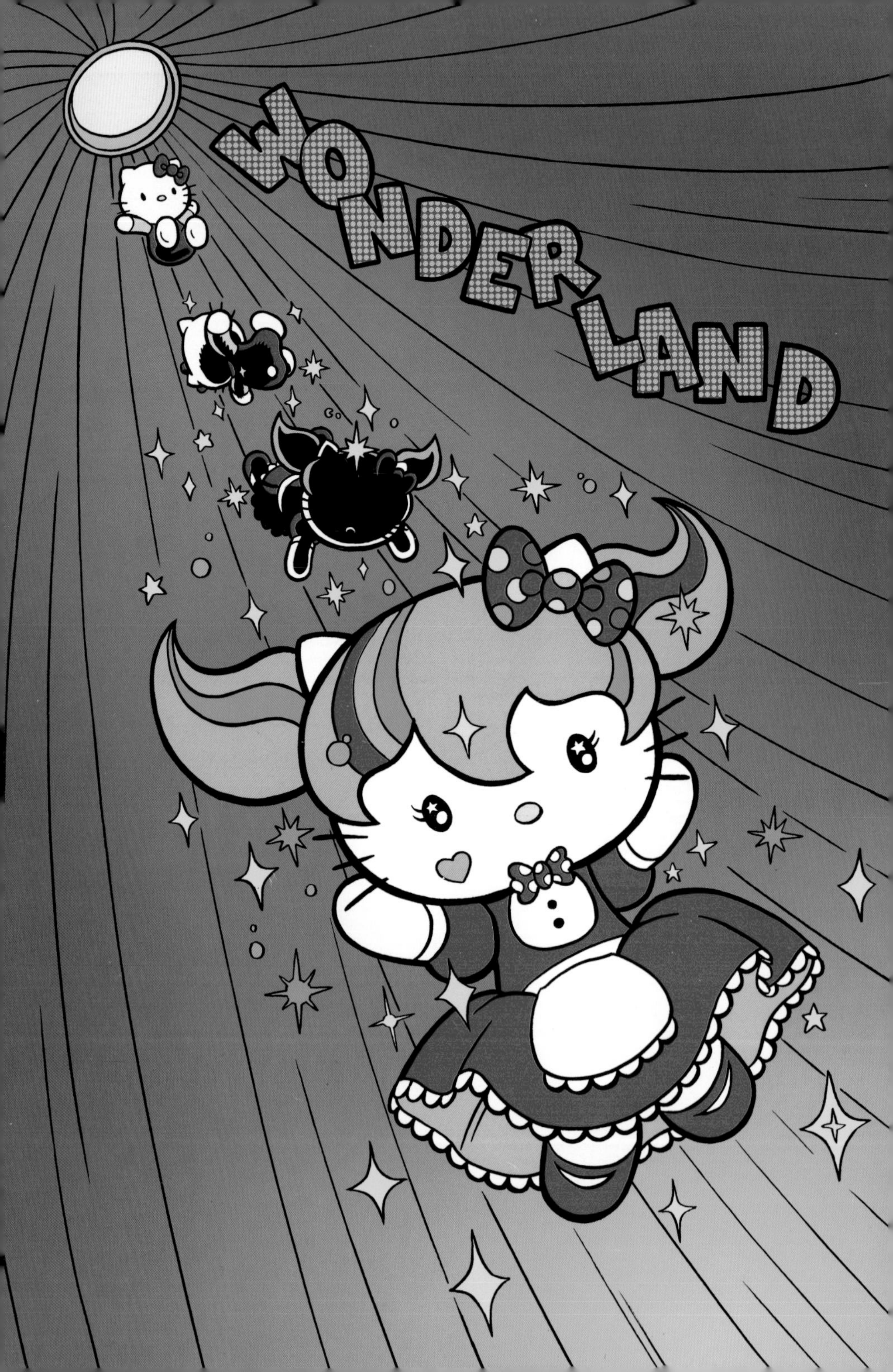
WONDERLAND

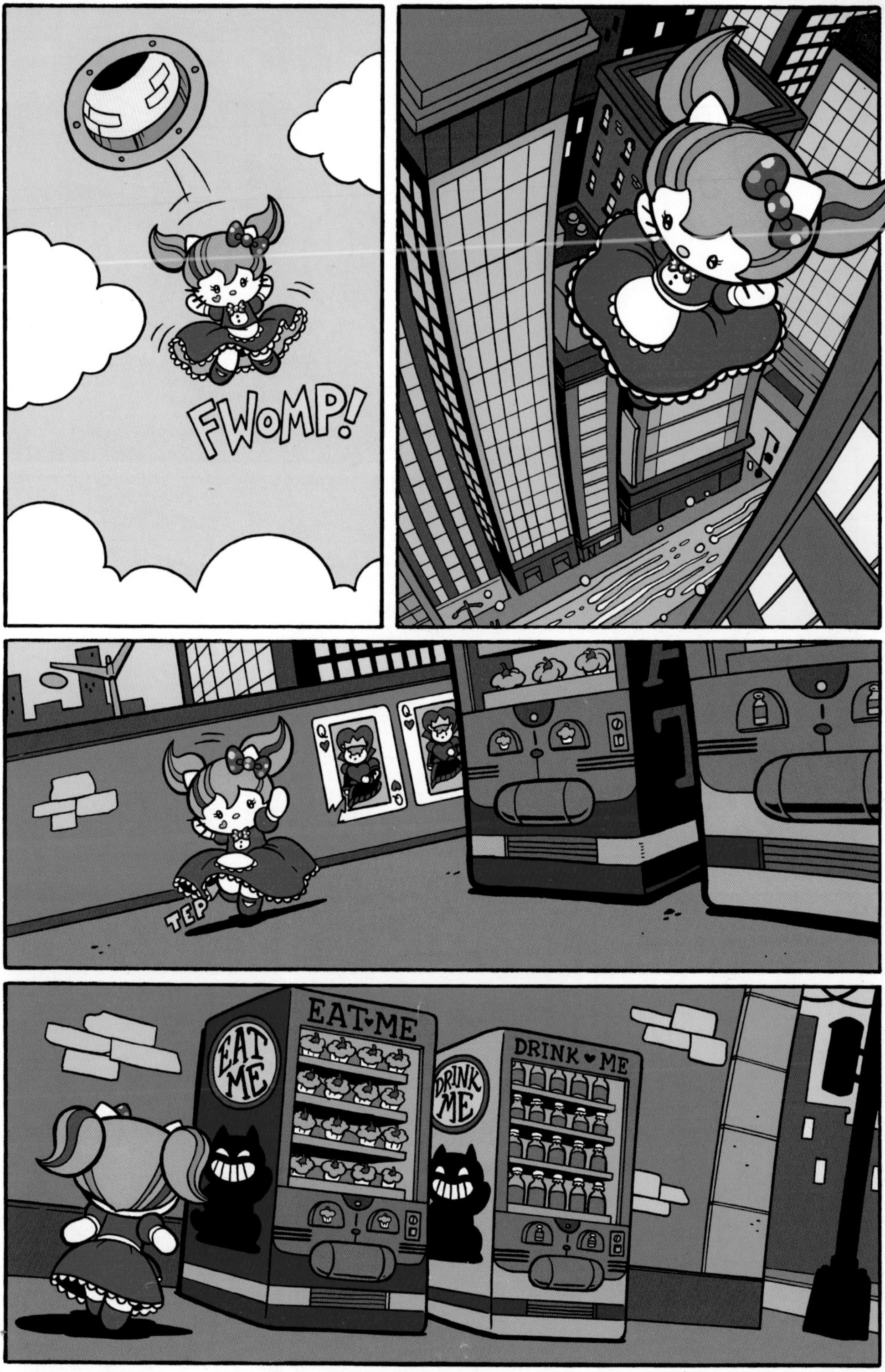
FWOMP!
TEP
EAT ME
EAT ME
DRINK ME
DRINK ME

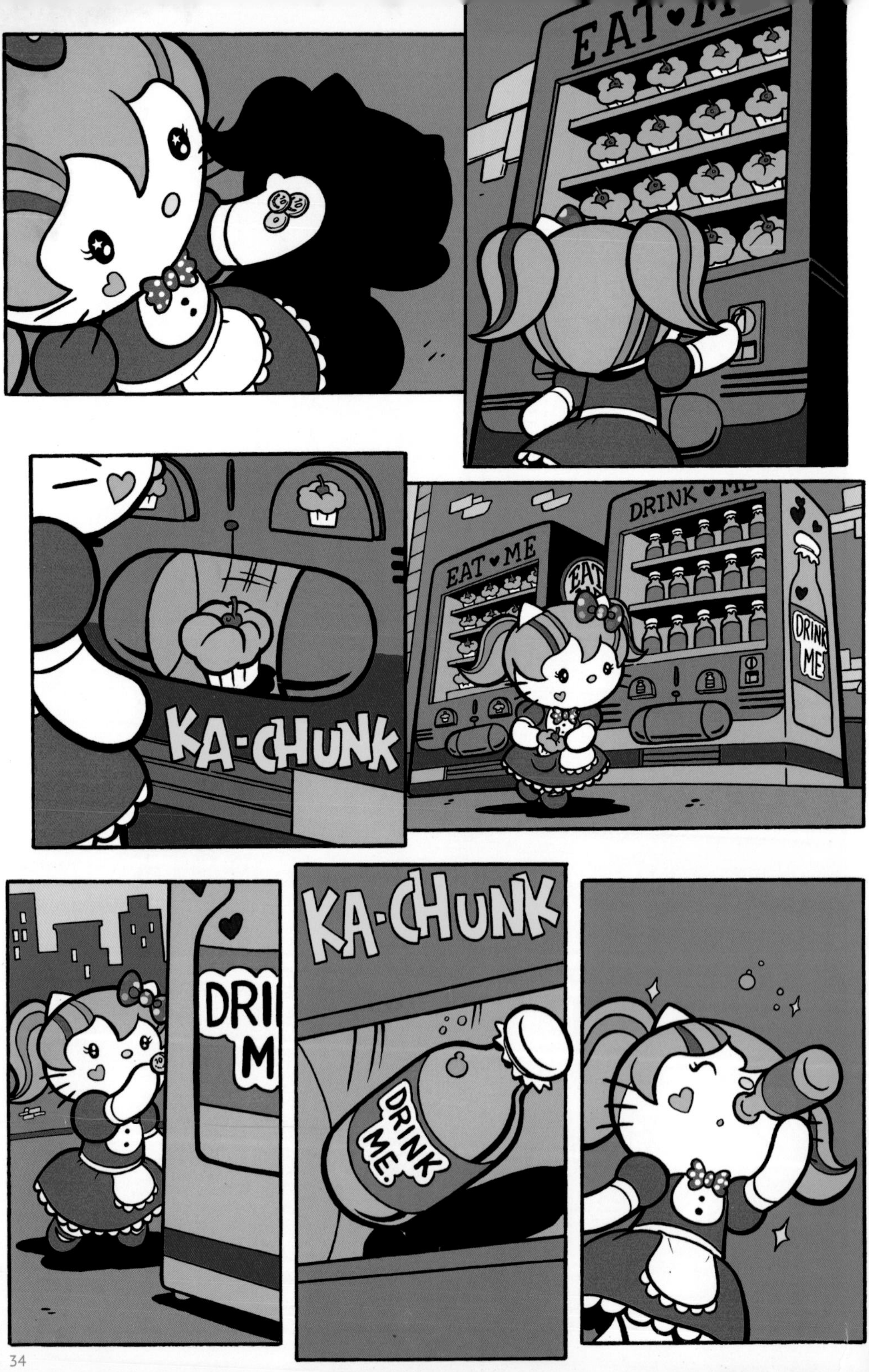

EAT ♥ ME
KA-CHUNK
EAT ♥ ME
DRINK ♥ ME
DRINK ME
DRI
M
KA-CHUNK
DRINK ME.

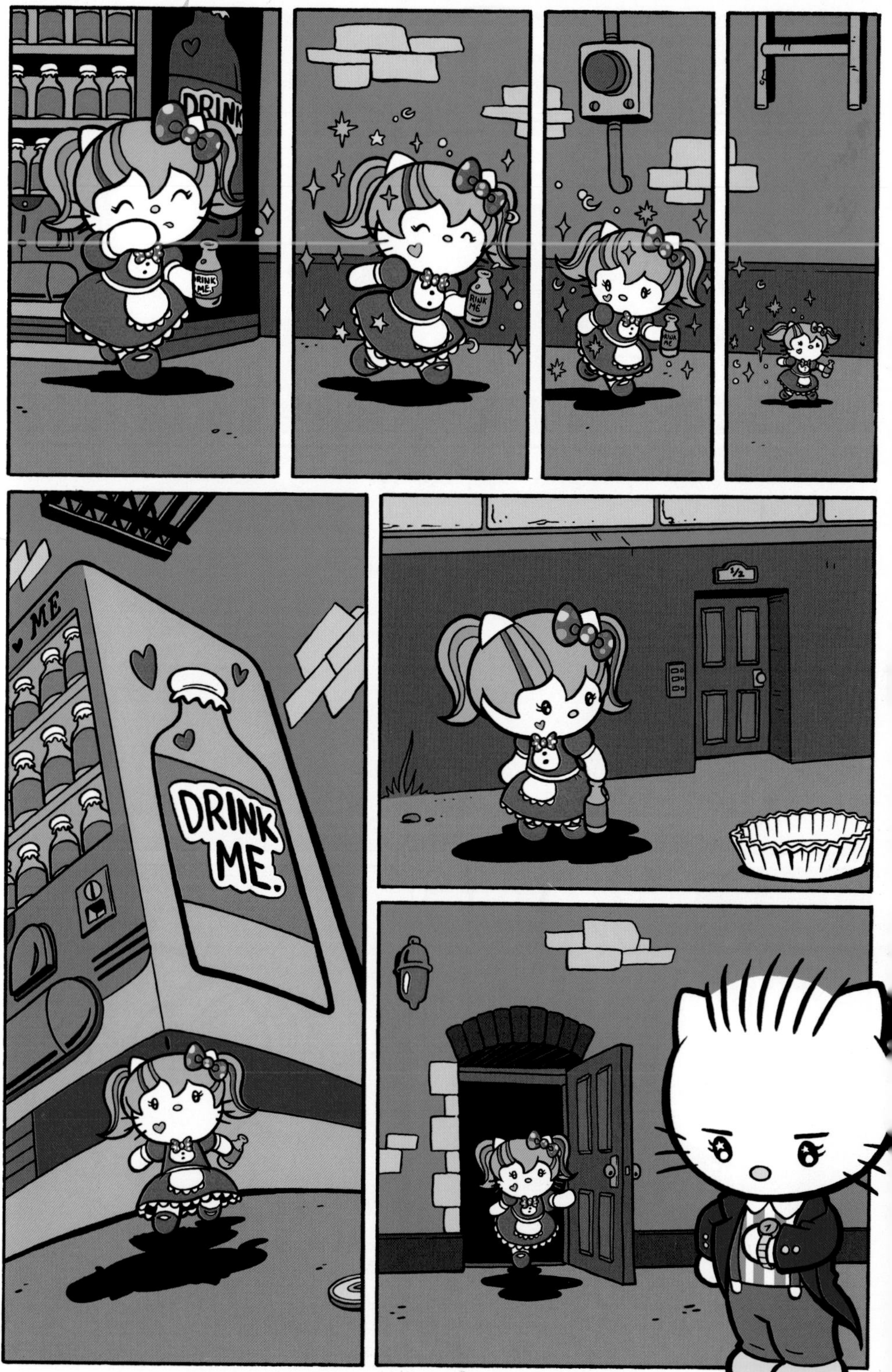

DRINK
DRINK ME.
DRINK ME
DRINK ME
ME
DRINK ME.
1/2

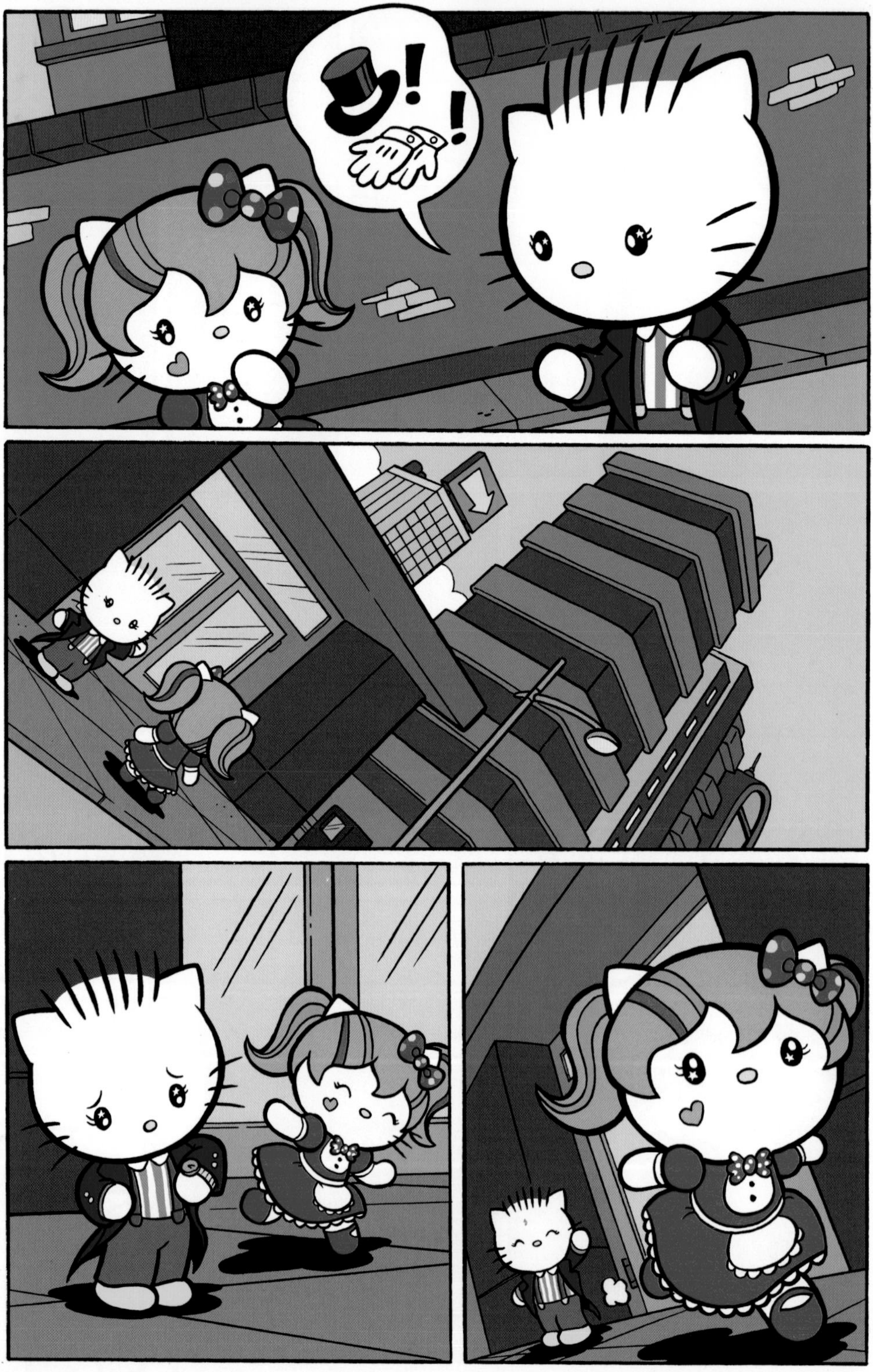
!
!

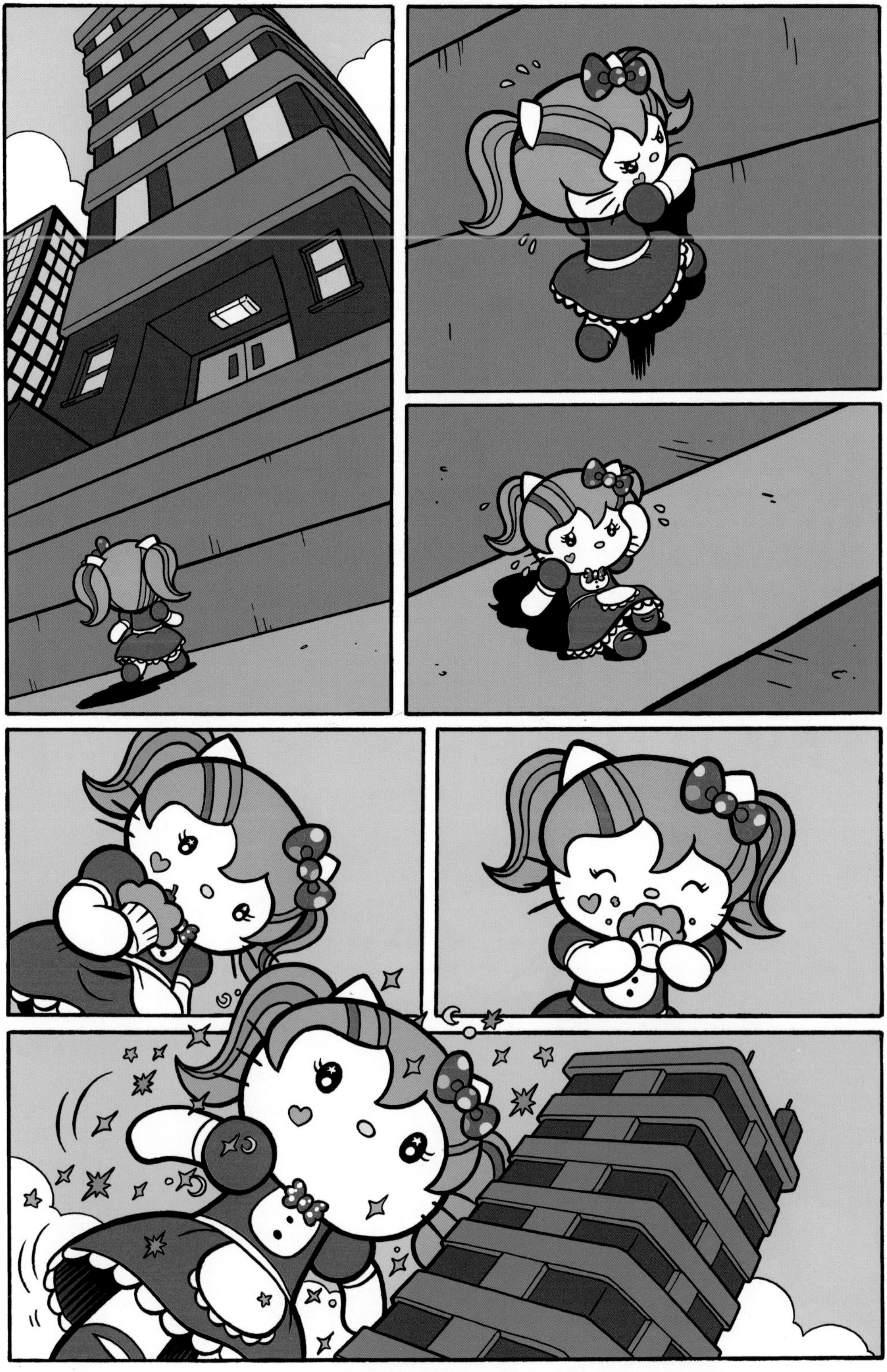

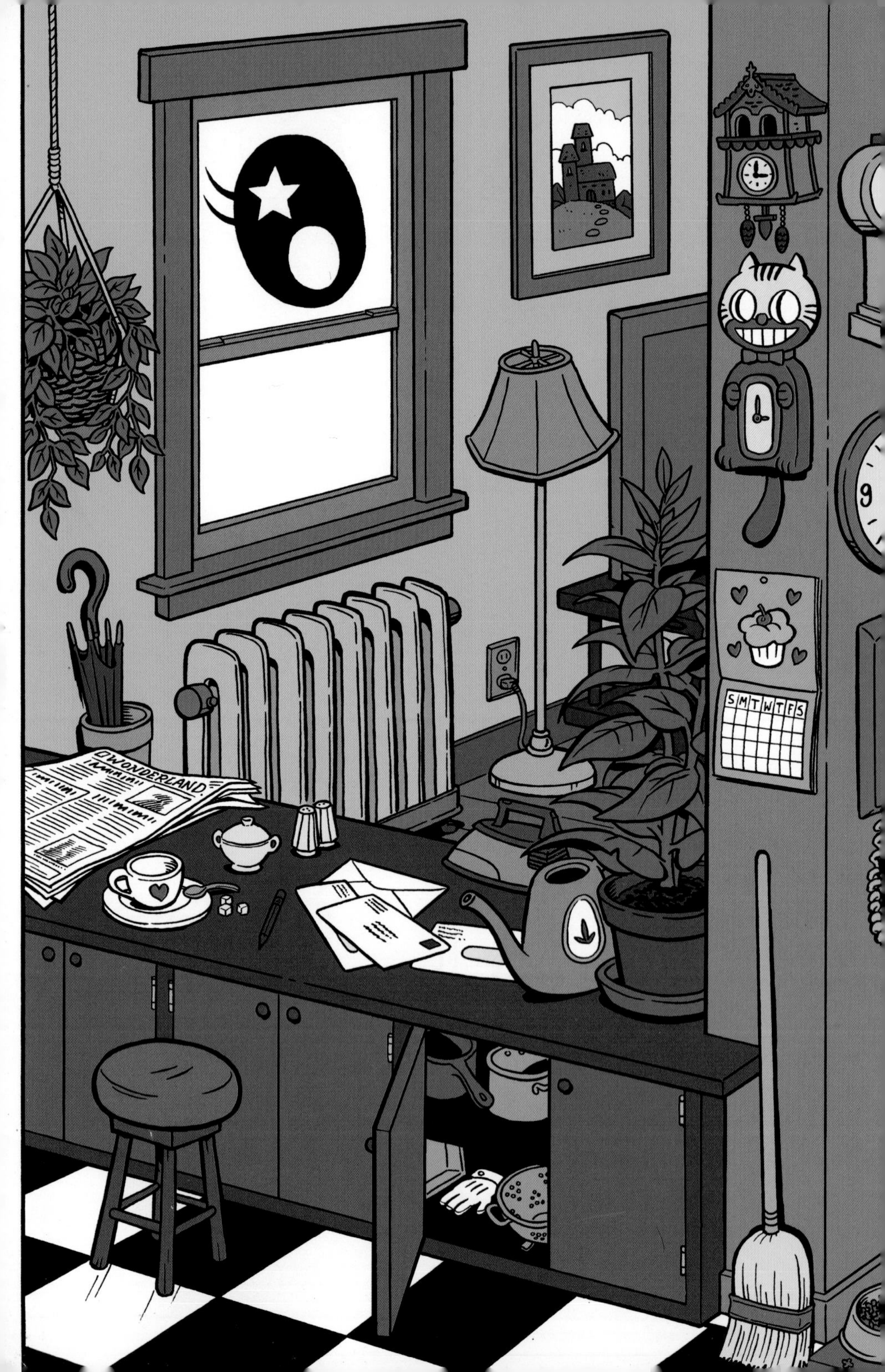
WONDERLAND
S M T W T F S

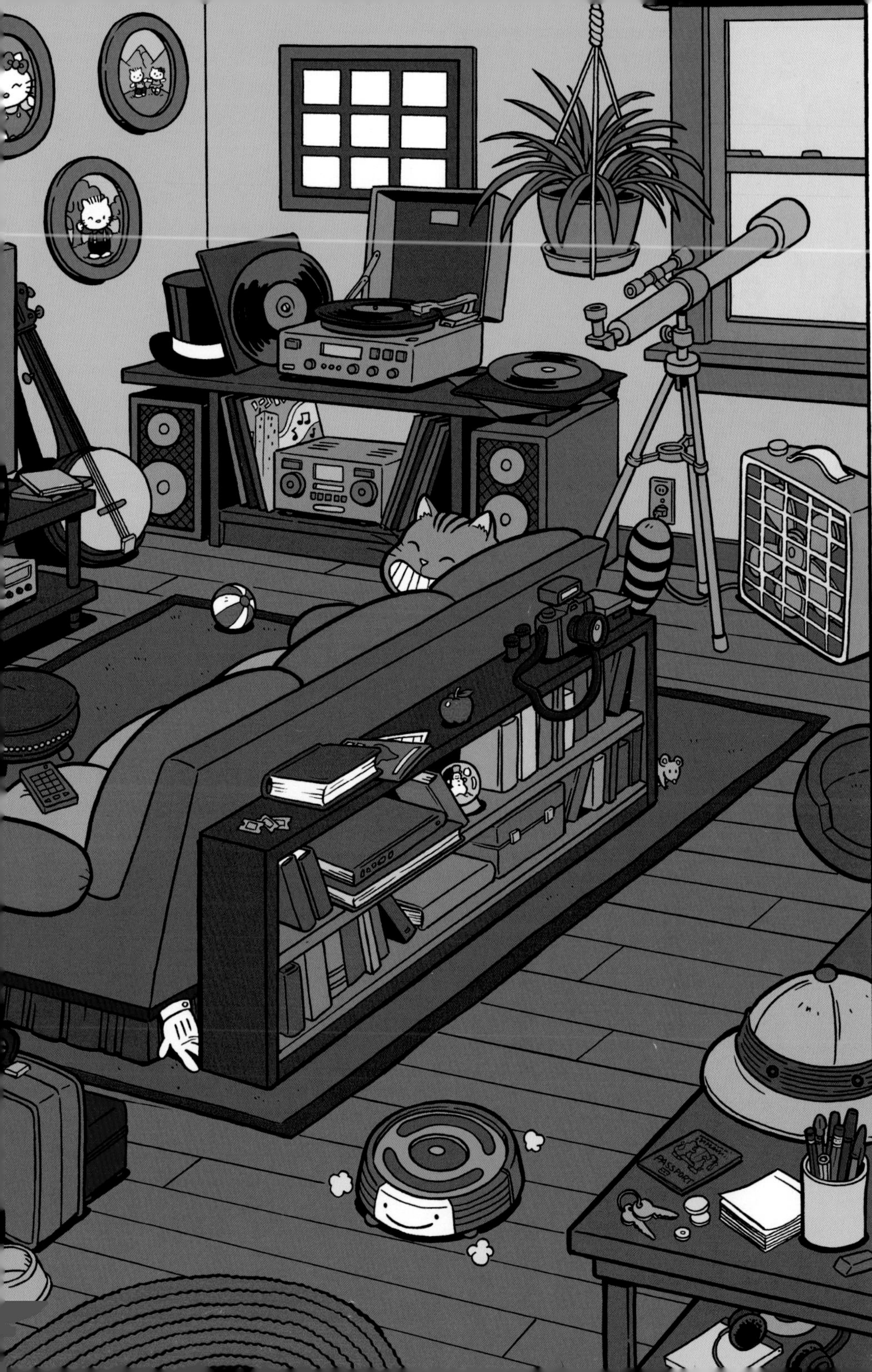
PASSPORT

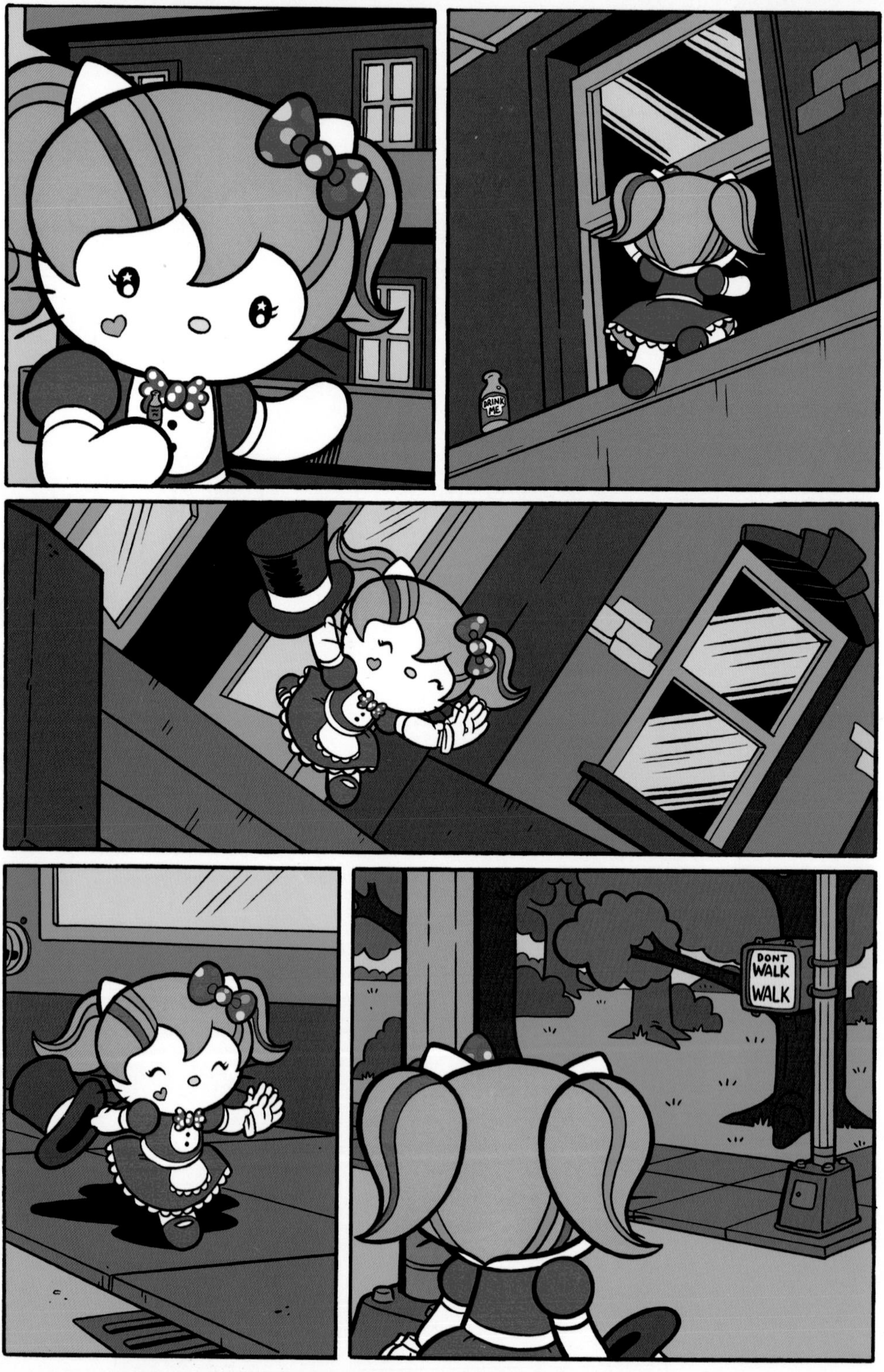
DRINK ME
DONT WALK
WALK

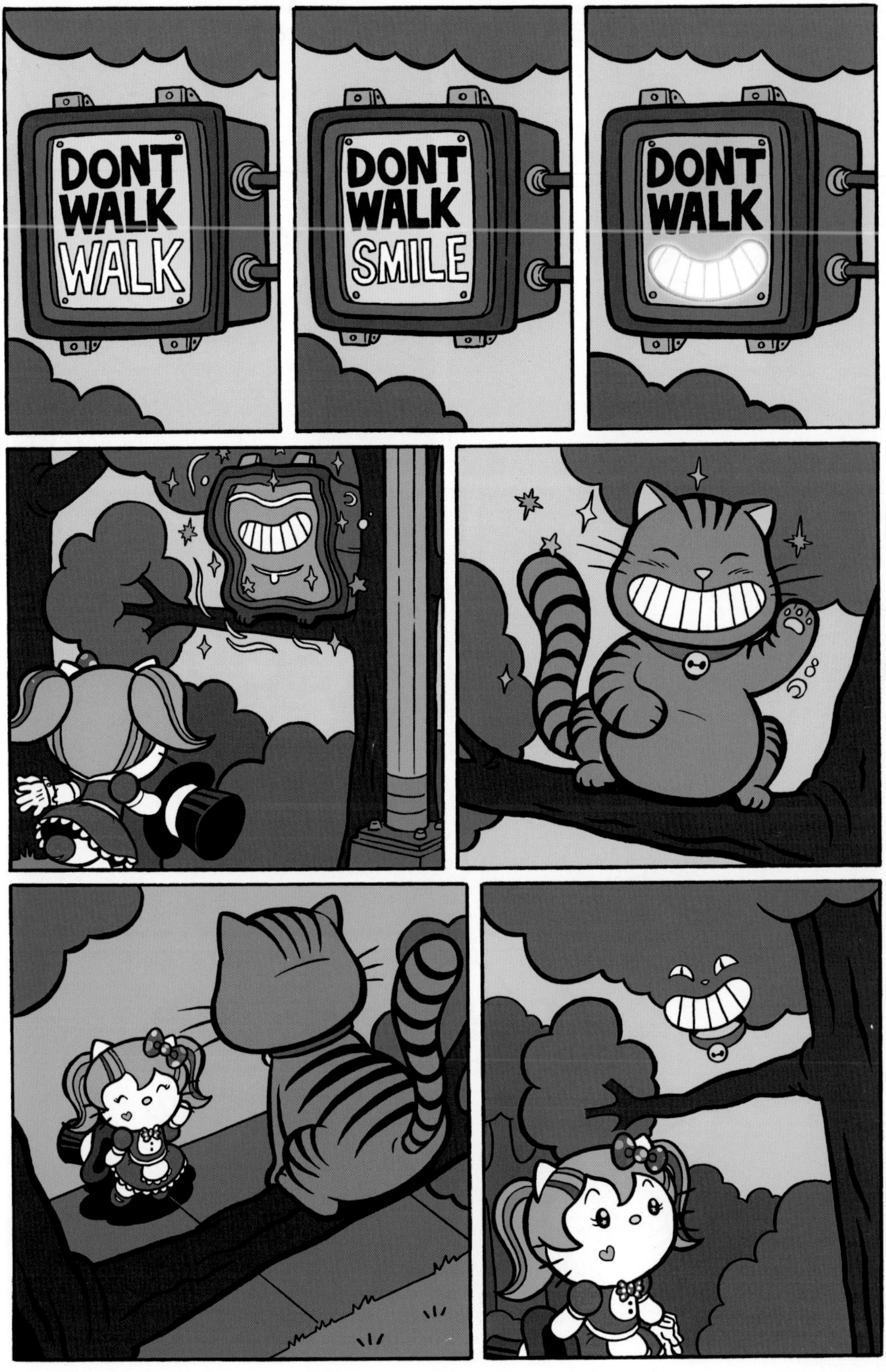
DONT WALK
WALK
DONT WALK
SMILE
DONT WALK

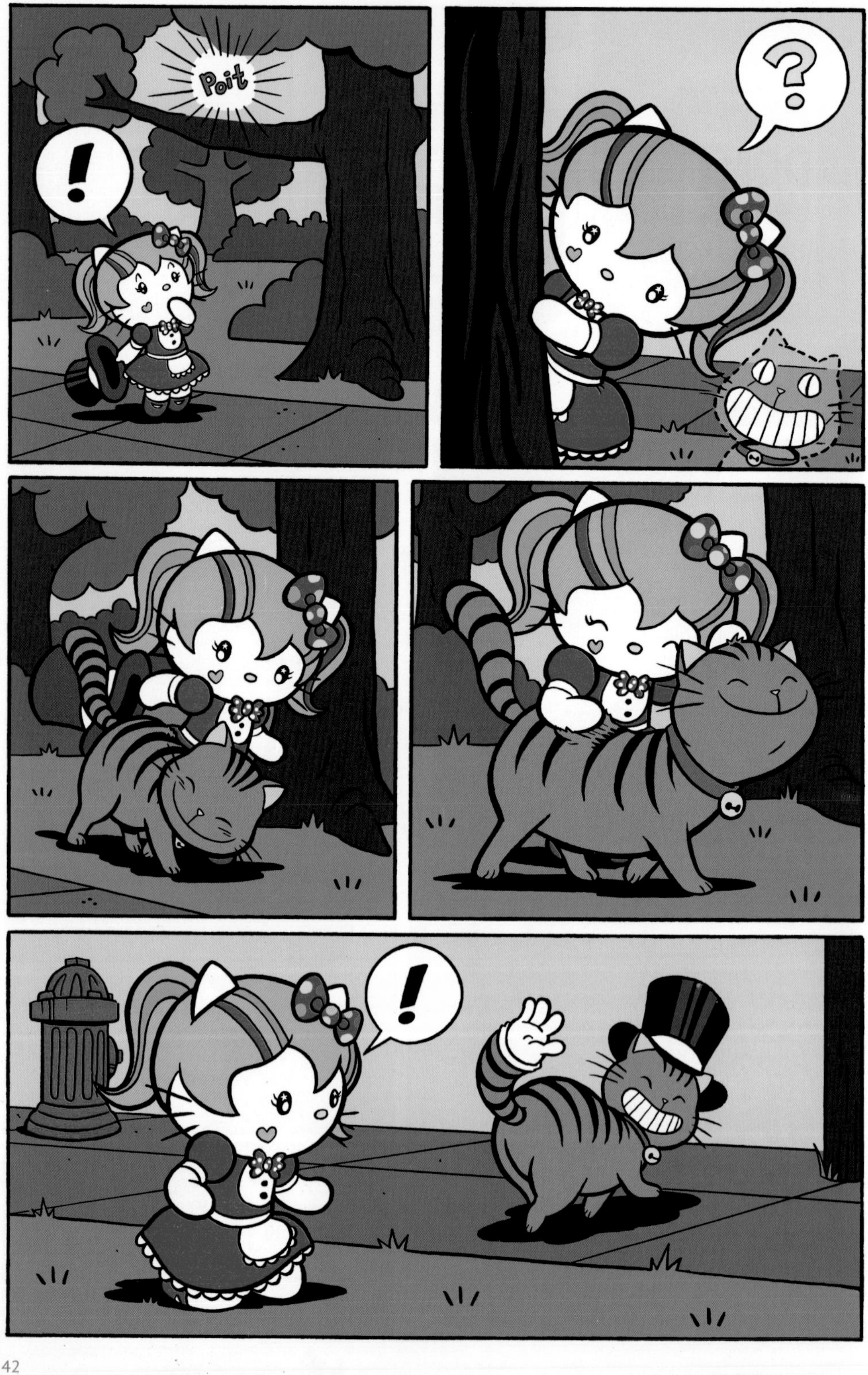
Poit
!
?
!

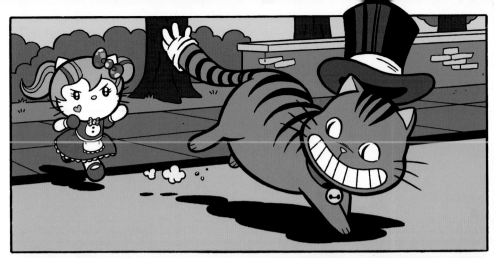

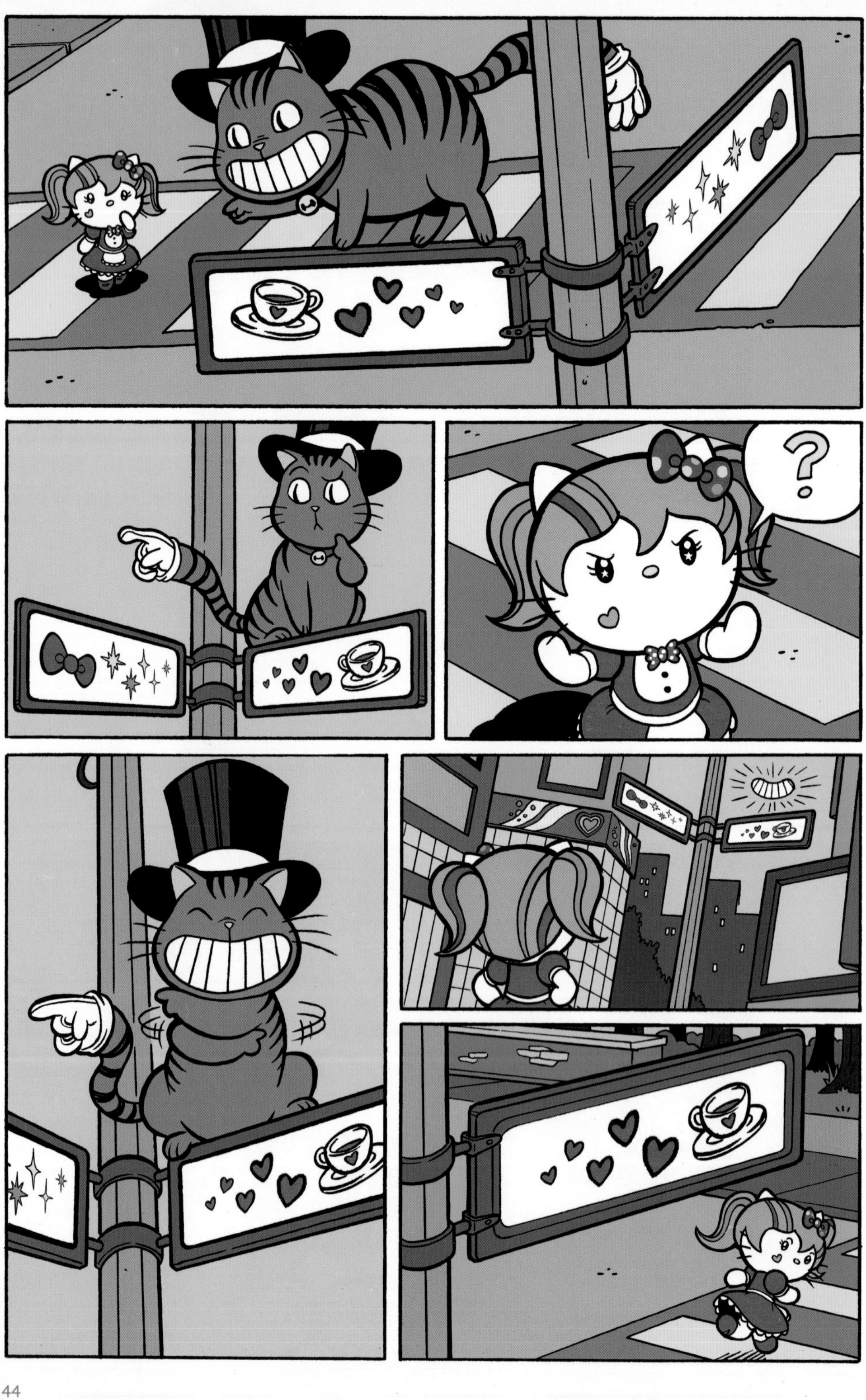
?

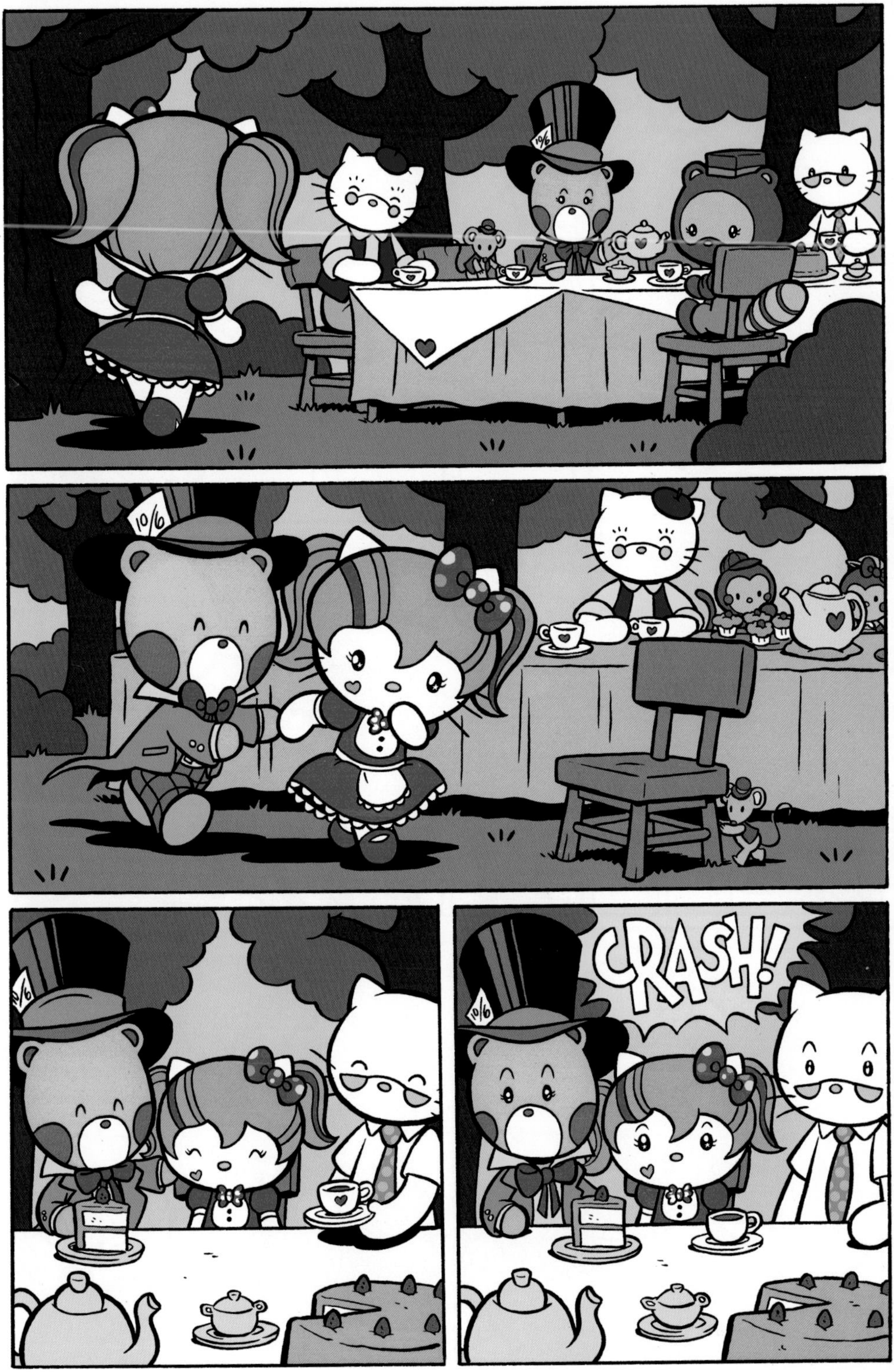
CRASH!

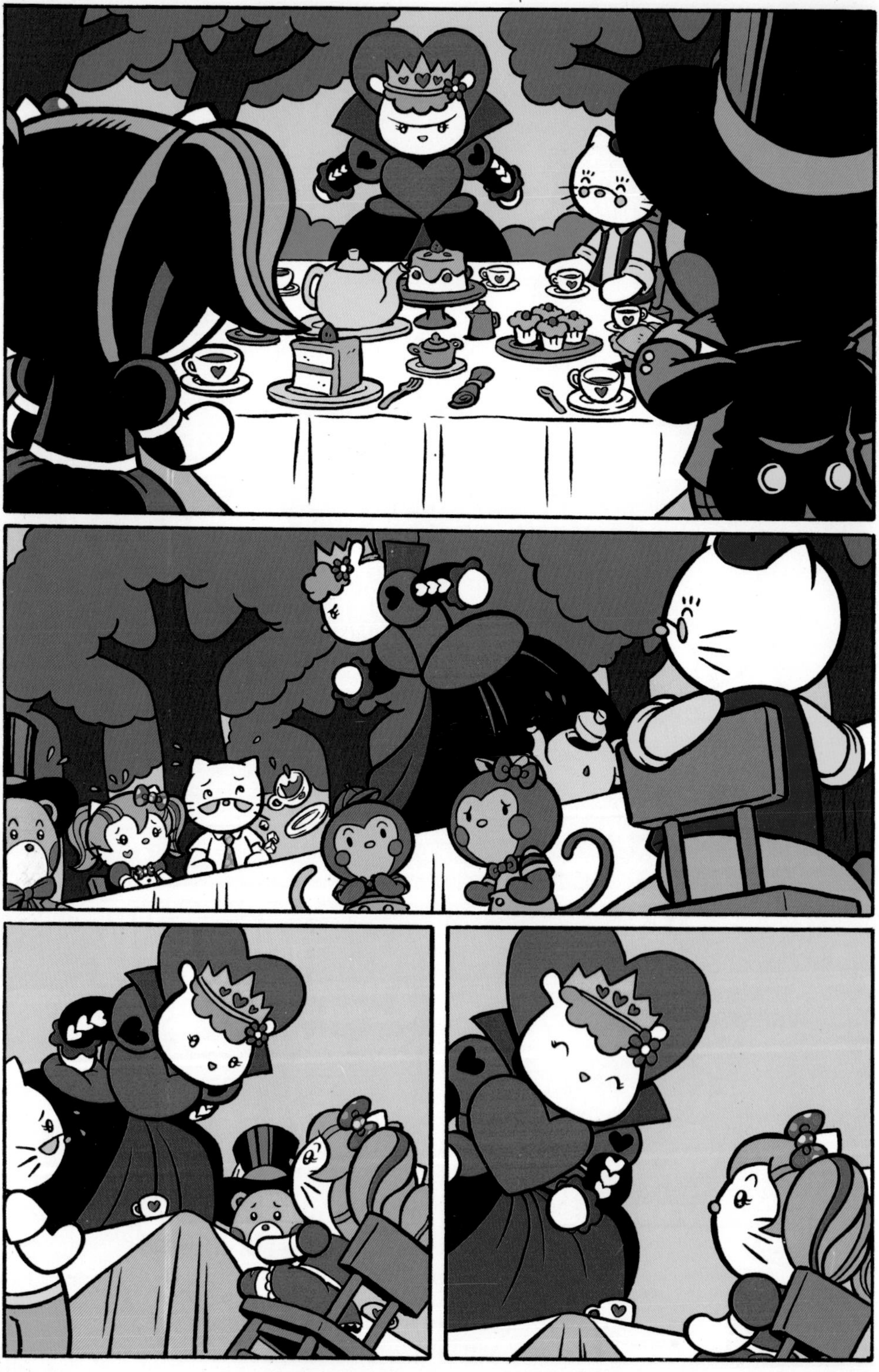

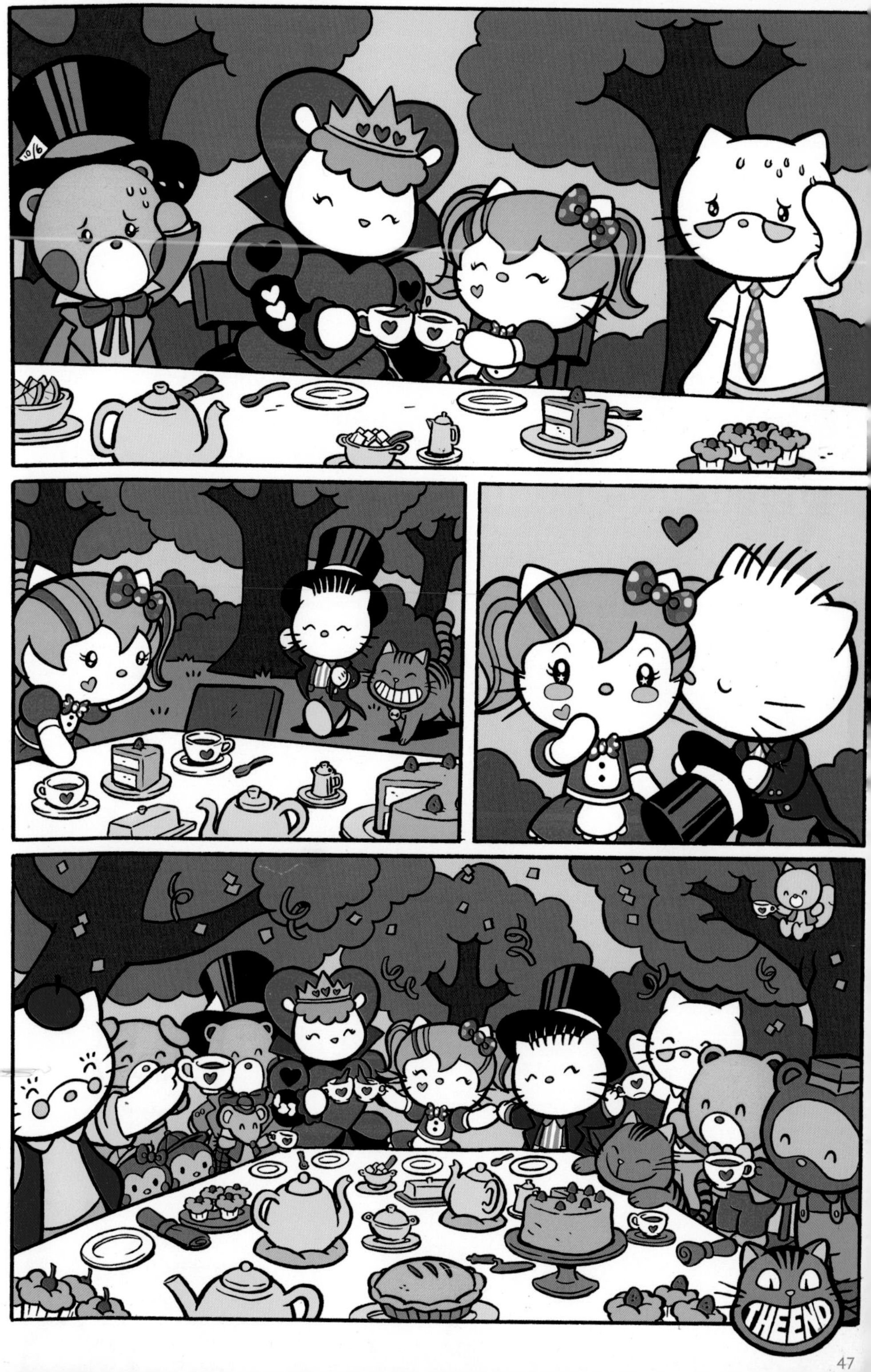
10/6
THE END

CREATORS

Jacob Chabot is a New York City-based cartoonist, illustrator and writer. His comics have appeared in publications such as *Nickelodeon Magazine, Mad Magazine, Spongebob Comics,* and various Marvel titles. He also illustrated *Voltron Force: Shelter from the Storm* and *Voltron Force: True Colors* for VIZ Media. His comic *The Mighty Skullboy Army* is published through Dark Horse and in 2008 was nominated for an Eisner Award for Best Book for Teens.

Victoria Maderna is an Argentinian illustrator currently living in Toledo, Spain, where she shares a studio and a life with her other half, who also happens to be an illustrator. She spends most of her time producing large quantities of pencil shavings and paint splatters in order to grow her books and comics collection. Animals are her favorite thing to draw. In her free time she also dabbles in gardening, writing and sewing silly creatures. Her work has appeared in magazines, children's books, games, comics and greeting cards.

Ian McGinty lives in Savannah, Georgia, and also parts of the universe! Also, Earth. When he isn't drawing comics and rad pictures of octopuses (octopi?), he's laughing at funny-looking dogs and making low-carb burritos! Ian draws stuff for VIZ Media, Top Shelf Productions, BOOM! Studios, Zenescope and many more cool folk! But he cannot draw garbage trucks for some reason.

Michael E. Wiggam is a professional comic book colorist whose work includes *Voltron Force* for VIZ Media, *Star Wars: Clone Wars* for Dark Horse Comics, Raymond E. Feist's *Magician Master: Enter the Great One* for Marvel Comics, *R.P.M.* and *I.C.E.* for 12 Gauge Comics, and various other publications. He was born and raised in Florida but has lived in Europe and seven U.S. states. Currently, he is earning an MFA from Savannah College of Art and Design.